CLOUDBURSTS

SHORT STORIES
AND PLAYS

BY

VELGEN

Published by Muddy Puddle Press
P O Box 97124
Lakewood W A 98497
www.valdumond.com

ISBN: 978-0-9887506-1-6

First edition

Printed in the United States of America

Library of Congress Cataloging-in-Publication Data:
Available from publisher
Val Dumond
Cloudbursts
Original short stories and plays
By Velgen (Val Dumond)
ISBN: 978-0-9887506-1-6

OTHER BOOKS BY VAL DUMOND

NONFICTION
The Anarchist's Guide to Grammar
Grammar For Grownups
Elements of Nonsexist Usage
Just Words — The Us and Them Thing
Imagine! Breathe! Write!
Are You Singing Your Song?
SHEIT — A No-nonsense Guidebook
to Writing and Using Nonsexist Language
Doin' the Puyallup
Steilacoom's Church
Olympia Coloring Book

FICTION
A Little Rebellion
When Roosters Fly
Sugar, Spice, and Stone
Ahlam's Stories
How We Fought World War II
at William T. Sherman Elementary School
Mush On and Smile (Klondike Kate)

ANTHOLOGY
The Sun Never Rises
Dream Makers

CONTENTS

DEDICATION

To my grownup adult
offspring (children),
Frederick and Lisbeth,
who keep their
mother
going.

And to my grownup adult
Granddaughter Kiona.

WHY THE CLOUDBURST?

"Ah, sweet mystery of life, at last I've found you" were the opening lines of a song popular when I was very young. It's taken many decades to discover their meaning. At last... I believe I've uncovered that mystery — or at least some of it.

For one, I have found the place to live that is perfect for me. After freezing in Wisconsin for twenty years, then roasting in Florida for another score, I wandered into the Pacific Northwest with its glorious mountains and sparkling waters. I now am dazzled by moderate winters, spectacular springs, comfortable summers, extravagant autumns, and by closeness with friends and family.

The most exciting part of my discovery is the time to write and the means to do it the way I want to. After years of writing, mostly for others, and teaching language and writing, my time is now mine to do with as I wish — and I wish to write. Somehow, I managed to write and publish a couple dozen books over my career, and now I have assembled the myriad short stories and plays written and stockpiled over a lifespan. I'm sharing some of them in this book with the hope you will enjoy reading them as much as I enjoyed writing them.

I didn't know I could write fiction, even though I was doing it. I thought that because I wrote for a living — for newspapers and magazines, for advertising agencies, and for businesses of all sizes — fiction was out of my league. Now, when I review some of the stories, I sometimes cannot remember where the ideas came from, whatever possessed me to write about... that?

Some of this work addresses subjects disturbing, to me as I wrote it and now read it, and probably to you as you read it. However, everything I include involves life with all its mysteries. Maybe not *all*. There are always more mysteries to uncover and write about.

The author's name may confuse you, especially if you know me or my previous work. Names are important. During my married years, I discovered an inability to write creatively while I carried someone else's name. When I reclaimed my family name, I again was able to satisfy my passion for writing.

Velgen is my given name, which I shed in my teens, mostly to avoid mispronunciations. I sheltered my name — knowing it is unique — until now. If I'm sharing my innermost expressions of life, why not share my innermost sense of being, my name? I wrote all the work in this book, except for two short items I found in public domain that seemed to fit. All work in this book is f-i-c-t-i-o-n!

The book title, *Cloudbursts*, reflects not only the first creative story I ever wrote, but explains my feeling for letting go, opening the life valve and letting the senses loose.

But sometimes when a cloud bursts, it releases surprises, like sleet in July, thunderstorms in January, tornados and cyclones. And other surprises, like welcome warm rain after a cold spell, drenching rain ending a drought, or rain that washes out your enemy's garden party (tee-hee). My writing portfolio is full; I needed a cloudburst to release its contents, whatever the outpouring.

Aah! Now that feels better.

SECTION I

AFTERWORDS

How to begin a collection of short stories that cover a random lot of ideas? Let's begin at the end, the expectations, the emotions, the regrets, and the prose about what happens when you have finished something — living perhaps.

In this section, you'll find stories about goodbyes and endings, along with obituaries of some different kinds of people. The aged seem fascinated with checking the obits in the newspaper to "see if I'm there; if I'm not, I begin my day."

Included are some stories about saying goodbye, endings of different natures. Philosophically, we all know that whatever begins must end in some way. With marriage, the choices are the Ds: Divorce, Desertion, Death. With careers, the Us: Uselessness, Unrealized expectation, Usury, Undoing. With love affairs, the Ts: Treachery, Tedium, Too much, Too little.

The common thread is expectation gone awry for one reason or another. You don't have to understand the reason to feel the loss.

How do you say goodbye? *So long, bye-bye, see you, adieu, adios, ta-ta, outa here, get out!* Oh, the choices are endless.

Here we begin a journey of discovery — for writing fiction is the greatest method of discovery ever devised by and for artists (that means you). Read, enjoy, turn the page, and begin to read about the end.

GET READY TO MEET YOUR MAKER

HOW?

When you're told to "prepare to meet your maker", what do you do? Who do you expect to meet? What will you wear? And just where will this all take place?

Will my maker wear a red carnation? Or a blue scarf? Will I recognize her/him/it? Will there be a gleam in my maker's eyes? Or will there even be eyes?

As for what to wear, do I wear black? white? something colorful with flowers? a dress? Can I get by with a pair of blue jeans? Clean of course, but jeans? Or would a neat pair of properly creased slacks do the job?

As for where this will take place, will it be "heaven"? And what is heaven? Where is it? How do I get there? Take the A-train or a jet plane? Would a bus take me that far? Or could I drive?

Just how do you prepare to meet your maker? My maker? Our maker? Ah, the questions!

HEATHER'S SOUL

"Where should I drop this Soul?"

"Don't you have your Soul schedule? Your route? What kind of Soul Power rep are you?"

"Sorry, boss. Sometimes I get so caught up with my work that I forget where I'm going. You know how it is."

"Actually, I don't. You have your instructions, Ergo. Now either stay with the program or…." The Power Chief didn't finish the sentence.

Ergo consulted her schedule, dropped the Soul, and the Powers continued to file other used Souls. Intermittently they would pull one out to drop into a new place. From where they sat, the Powers could see all of time and every inch of space, particularly Earth. Their jobs required it.

I suppose you know that sometimes the Powers just plain make mistakes. They're not supposed to, which accounts for the intricate filing system, but mistakes do happen. Like when the swan's egg got placed in the duck's nest, or when the artist fell into a dreary mining town, or when the boy was raised by a pack of wolves. Jewels sometimes tumble into stony outbacks or coal fields. It happens. Just as hobos land inside spacious, decorated palaces. Mistakes.

Heather always knew who she was. It was the world she had fallen into that troubled her. Time and place had seemed skewed from the beginning. She often fantasized about who she truly was and where she ought to live.

"Hollywood. Yes, that would be a good place for me. Or maybe New York," she thought. "Or perhaps I should live in London… Paris… Hong Kong… or the mountains." Her terms would turn generic, "or a rain forest… or the desert…"

"Then again… what if this is the wrong time?" she mused. But at what better time should she have lived? Fifty years earlier? The Holy Wars? The Renaissance? Frontier-expanding America in the 1800s? The age of the Incas? Or the future, when she could wander freely around the Universe?

"Nonsense," the young woman told herself. "Right time, right place. Maybe… just maybe… I'd do better as someone else. That's it, I should've been… let's see, Joan of Arc. Or Amelia Earhart. Or Eleanor Roosevelt. Or Queen Victoria of the British Empire. Or a heron. Or…" she hesitated a moment before adding, "a dance teacher in Peoria, Illinois."

Heather mused; the Powers continued their filing. "Hmmm," the Power Chief approached, humming and holding up a folder that bulged with files. "Isn't this the Soul that you claimed was worn out by so much use? I thought you were going to give this one a rest."

"Let me see." The fumbling Ergo grabbed the folder and began to read. After a moment, she looked up, a sheepish smile on her face. "Sorry, boss. I remember now that the Power Board agreed to put this one to rest for a time. But…"

"This better be good."

"Well, we noticed this call for a Soul and… the circumstances seemed so special… so… yes, that's the word… special. We couldn't resist."

"I don't remember any…"

"You were on R&R that week. I guess we forgot to mention this one."

"What were the… special circumstances?"

"We simply realized this little girl needed a well-used Soul, one that had seen some great moments. This one — the one used by Joan of Arc, that flier Earhart, Mrs. Roosevelt, and Mrs. Kennedy — well, it just seemed…"

"But notice also, Ergo, that this what-you-call *special soul* had also been used by Queen Victoria, a heron, and that dancer in Peoria."

"I know. Well," Ergo harrumphed and hesitated before she said, "We were thinking of retiring this much-used Soul after one more round. We probably should have retired it before the Peoria woman. But you see, boss, we knew this little girl was a writer. Since we'd given her the Itchy Writer Syndrome, we figured she'd need some backup, you know, some… experience… something to write about. So…"

Ergo waited to be chastised. But all she heard was the chuckle of approval from the Power Chief who slowly walked away.

"Well done, Ergo," came the faint call from down the hallway. "Well done."

OBITUARIES OF THE RICHLY FAIRY-TALED

King Charming

King Charming succumbed today at the age of 92, leaving his wife Queen Snow White to rule the nation of Fiction. Charming was the son of Queen Tarts and her consort, Jack Tarts. His death occurred last evening after presiding at a banquet celebrating the opening of a new branch of his housecleaning business, CleanUrAshes.

The former Prince Charming was raised in royalty without having to earn a living, but in later years chose to honor his wife with a business. His accomplishments over his long lifetime include… well… finding a wife, marrying her, ascending to the throne, and… opening the business at Queen Snow's request. The queen was seeking a way to help her dwarf friends escape the deadly mines.

He had few other accomplishments in his life. He was father to a son and a daughter, grandpa to a passel of grandchildren and a mess of great grandchildren.

King Charming has become well known for his vast collection of newspaper clippings that recount the stories and demises of many residents of the nation of Fiction. Some of these are included in the on-line version of this obituary. Go to: KingCharming.com for more details.

King Charming is survived by his queen, Snow White; their two children, Prince Charming Jr. (Princess Cinderella), and Princess Ellafitz; and the queen's stepmother Wicked. Queen Snow White is expected to continue to rule the land of Fiction.

Services will be held at the palace for family only, since the king never bothered to make friends. Burial will be in the family tomb in The Woods. Contributions in lieu of flowers may be made to Seven Dwarfs Mining Company.

[With the generous permission of the Internet, the following obituaries reflect the kind found in King Charming's collection.]

Goldie Lochs

Famed real estate agent Goldie Lochs was found dead in her home Tuesday after suffering injuries due to a severe beating. Her wounds indicated a confrontation with a large intruder. Police are following leads through remnants of hair found at the scene and fingerprints made by traces of honey. Ms. Lochs was 42.

Ms. Lochs became a real estate agent long before messing up a major transaction and entering a long period in her life of breaking and entering. When arrested, she said she was building her real estate business by taking advantage of empty homes. It seems she preferred to use these homes in lieu of spending money for her own home.

After serving a prison term of eighteen months in a privately owned institution, Ms. Lochs was released on her own recognizance. While in prison, she led fellow inmates through cooking classes where she taught them to make bear claws. Within weeks of her release, she was back in the real estate business, this time operating solely from an office (which doubled as living quarters).

Police Chief Bayer S. Perin has called Ms. Lochs' death a murder and is pursuing suspects throughout the area, focusing on the heavily forested area near the mountains. Funeral services are pending.

Ms. Lochs is survived by her parents, Smokey and Kareem Lochs. She had no siblings, and her grandparents gave up on her many years ago, preferring to move away rather than endure one more telling of her story about an encounter with bears in the forest.

Scarlett "Little Red" Ridinghood

Target Store's spokesperson announced today the death of Scarlett "Little Red" Ridinghood, who recovered from childhood trauma to become a model and representative for the company. Her identity with the company's red logo was well known in the advertising business.

Little Red was hired as Target's spokeswoman after ten years as a New York model. The charming Little Red took her name from her penchant for wearing red clothing. The trademark earned her a reputation among advertisers and landed her the job with Target. Her death allegedly occurred from an overdose of "those little red pills". She was 39.

Ms. Ridinghood had survived several death threats by an angry business tycoon, Cyril T. Lobo, who claimed she was mentally ill. She accused him of following her to grandmother's home in The Woods and attacking her when she was a teenager. She claimed the businessman gained access to the gated community and forced his way into the Ridinghood home. He was arrested and released without charges.

Ms. Ridinghood's life was fraught with sadness. She lost her parents when she was twelve and her grandmother about five years later. The grandmother succumbed to heart failure after an attack in her home. Little Red took herself to the Big Apple and turned to modeling after attempting a brief acting career.

Funeral services will be held at Target Store headquarters for close friends. Ms. Ridinghood has no surviving family.

Huffenpuff Wolf

Huffenpuff Wolf has succumbed from an asthma attack at 64, after retiring to the Home for Vagrant Wolves in Olympia, Washington. He was well known in the area as a bill collector who could get the job done without violence.

Mr. Wolf was born to Beyo and Grey Wolf, in the mountainous region of northern Canada and raised by humans in White Horse. He entered the United States during a period when wolves were protected by law, but later was captured and taken to a farm in Washington where he was displayed to the public alongside a variety of wolfish creatures.

In his youth, he was accused of harassing a teenage girl in The Woods, but the accusations were proven false. Mr. Wolf filed a counter suit against the girl, but it was thrown own of court by "a biased judge", according to Mr. Wolf.

Mr. Wolf escaped the Washington compound about fifteen years ago and took a turn at bill collecting. His employers found Mr. Wolf an asset to the company and paid him well to frighten homeowners out of their dwellings.

He drew the attention of the Associated Press about nine years ago when he used his mighty lungs to destroy two homes belonging to a pot bellied pig and a wild boar. However, in pursuing a third homeowner, Mr. Wolf blew out his lungs and fell to the ravages of asthma.

Recaptured, he was confined to the Home for Vagrant Wolves, where he died Saturday. Plans for a memorial service are pending. Where do you bury a bill collecting wolf?

Princess Cinderella

The beautiful Princess Cinderella has died of exhaustion at 47, the result of confinement in her castle where she became the mother of eight children and grandmother of twenty-three. Some claim the castle proved more of a cage than her former life with her stepmother.

Following the loss of her mother, the princess remained with her father and his new family. She toiled in their home until she met Prince Charming Jr., son of the late King Charming and Queen Snow White. After a romantic search to identify the beautiful intruder to a palace ball, Junior Charming found his great love scrubbing fireplaces at her home.

The prince carried his princess back to the castle, where the young couple produced their eight daughters in as many years, five who survive the princess: Pearl, twins Jewel and Jade, Ruby, and Amethyst. Princess Cinderella is survived also by her husband, Prince Charming Jr., twenty-three grandchildren, her stepmother Spiteful, and two stepsisters, Ugly and Incontinent. Her parents and three children preceded her in death.

Prince Charming has announced a week of mourning for his wife, which includes closure of his inherited housecleaning business, CleanUrAshes. Funeral services will be confined to the castle and the family.

Prince Charming Jr.

Prince Charming, Jr. famed singer and son of the late King Charming and Queen Snow White, was found dead in a Hollywood palace yesterday after suffering a bout with the flu.

He had completed a longer than usual performance at the Rialto Theater the night before and was complaining of a sore throat. The husband of the late Princess Cinderella had just turned 60.

Junior Charming bought his way into Hollywood as a young man. He became an international singing idol, traveling the world and visiting his home castle about once a year (eight times). His wife, Princess Cinderella, preceded him in death thirteen years ago.

The prince was well loved by those who knew him, although he kept himself aloof from close relationships. He was known for his flights of fancy, his love of dancing and song, and his strong sense of independence.

A singer of popular music, Junior loved to add the old songs, music from folklore, to his shows. A romantic all his life, he became a novelist and wrote several romance stories under a pseudonym, turning over royalties to an unidentified home for unwed mothers.

The prince is survived by his sister, Princess Ellafitz, five of his eight children, thirty-six grandchildren, and his business manager, Anthony Goze.

Dough Boy

(By Anonymous, 2002)

It is with the saddest heart that I pass on the following news. Please join me in remembering a great icon, the veteran Pillsbury icon. The Pillsbury Doughboy died yesterday of a yeast infection and complications from repeated pokes in the belly. He had just turned 50, according to Doughboy's current spokesman, JoBe Cerny.

Doughboy was born from the creative minds of ad copywriter Rudy Perz and artist Martin Nodell, in early 1962, birthed on a kitchen table, right out of the oven.

Long-time friend Aunt Jemima, who delivered the eulogy, described Doughboy as a man who never knew how much he was kneaded. Doughboy rose quickly in show business, but his later life was filled with turnovers. He was not considered a very smart cookie, wasting much of his dough on half-baked schemes. Despite being a little flaky at times, he still, as a crusty old man, was considered a roll model for millions. Toward the end, it was thought he would rise again, but alas, he was no tart.

Dozens of celebrities turned out to pay their respects, including Mrs. Butterworth, Hungry Jack, the California Raisins, Betty Crocker, the Hostess Twinkies, Skippy, Jolly Green Giant, Morton Salt, Count Chocula, and Captain Crunch. The gravesite was piled high with flours.

Doughboy, also remembered as Pop N Serve and Pop N Fresh, will be buried in a lightly greased coffin. The funeral is set at 3:50 for about 20 minutes.

Doughboy is survived by his wife, Poppie Fresh (AKA Mrs. Poppin' Fresh, Pillsbury Doughgirl). Doughboy leaves behind four children, Play Dough, John Dough, Jane Dough, and Dosey Dough, plus one in the oven, to be named Bun-Bun. He is also survived by his grandparents,

6

Grandpopper and Granmommer; his Uncle Rollie, his elderly father, Pop Tart, and his beloved pets, Flapjack and Biscuit.

[Velgen compiled several of the "Dough Boy obits" that have appeared over the years, the earliest in 2002. You may pass this on to share the Dough Boy smile with someone else who may be having a crumby day and kneads it.]

SURVIVING

Surviving is what we do. We can't survive if we give up. What is the opposite of survival? Giving up? What does that lead to? If not extinction, then death. But that happens to all of us, doesn't it? Death.

I want to tell you about two women I have known, not all that well, but I have known them — because they were me. They are me. I am them. I write. They wrote. They wrote powerful words, wondrous words, telling words. They put together words as few can. They wrote every day, intensely, prolifically, endlessly. Endlessly. Is that survival?

Both were fighting illness as they aged. Both were full of life, having lived meaningful lives. But then, whenever is a life not full of meaning? Both were intent on telling their stories — writing them. They were intent on sharing them with others, the world.

Now it's my story. I must tell it, for I'm the one left. Oh, I know there are others who survive to tell their stories, but this one is mine to tell. And if I don't tell it, who will? I only pray that I survive long enough to get it down.

Then I pray that somehow, their stories and all the other stories of surviving women will get told... somehow.

My story isn't very different from theirs. Oh hell, it is completely different. I want to write that story, the one that will capture hearts and minds forever. I want to write that story that somehow eludes me. I wish I had the poetry of a Toni Morrison, the storytelling ability of a Barbara Kingsolver, the word prowess of an Emily Dickenson — you know, one of those people who draw words out of their heads that you marvel at or have to look up in dictionaries.

How are we different? I am here with time to write my words; they are not.

Here I am, in the position of writing a piece that will border on poetry in order to recount the beauty of two women who were survivors who didn't survive. Or did they?

That's the irony. No one survives forever. One can only survive an event — for a while — until one doesn't survive anymore. One cannot escape losing the survival game.

One of the women of whom I speak (god, I hate that who/whom stuff) was an artist. No, I will use the present tense. She is an artist. Just because her body is gone doesn't mean she has ceased to be. She is an artist. She spent… (another mean, nasty word to describe living) …she lived much of her life in an artist's studio, painting, drawing, creating beauty.

She used her creativity in many forms besides painting and drawing — weaving, cooking, baking, molding, shaping, building, encouraging, inspiring, teaching, and arranging. She used her creativity… period.

BettyMae, who called herself Bmae or just B, was brought up by her Greek family, fell in love with a handsome Danish-American naval officer, and toured the world with him, absorbing the grandiosity of the world and its wonders. For a time, she settled in her own art studio, where she welcomed others to share her artistic bounty. She loved that, the sharing.

Like many women of her time, Bmae didn't attach a lot of value to her work, other than its "intrinsic" value, the excitement of creation. We used that word "intrinsic" a lot in those days to rationalize a woman's audacity at entering a man's world. Few women held themselves in high enough esteem to dare to call their work "art". How many women artists can you name? (Besides Georgia O'Keefe?)

Bmae and her family (she had created three beautiful little daughters) moved to Northwest America where they were awed by the great mountains, the blustery bountiful sea, an array of flowers and fauna that seemed endless, and the lofty trees — green, fluffy, tall, ever-so-tall — that pointed to the heavens.

Look how the trees survive! That is Bmae's story, the why and how of trees that grow tall through the chaos of gales and constant wind, through fires that follow the lightning, through floods and heavy rains, and finally through the saws of timber cutters who try to hack them all away. "And still the tall fir grows". But she didn't write about the trees. She wrote about the humans who lived among them, the men and women who came to the trees to begin new lives and to raise their families. She wrote specifically about a Danish man who discovered the Northwest in the late 19th century, while serving on a whaling ship, how he brought his wife to share the beauty and raise their children. She wrote of survival — like the trees — at its most intense.

The other woman I want to tell you about is a mother who brought her only son to Canada to escape the mayhem of her native country, Iraq, in the early 21st century. For generations, her family had grown up along the beautiful banks of the Tigris — that ancient river which ran through her arid country and produced the life force for trees and flowers that some consider to be the Garden of Eden of the Christian Bible, the Garden of Allah in the Muslim Quran, and the Garden of the Jewish Torah.

Considered the home of civilization, her country has been fought over for centuries. One power after another has tried to control the lush, fertile place in the world that promised abundance and riches. And this woman had survived several of those attempts during her lifetime.

Her name, Ahlam, in Arabic means *dreams, visionary, witty, and imaginative.* Growing up in a charming small town south of Baghdad, she played games and ran free until she became a young woman. She learned the ways of Arabic women, donned the traditional scarf in public, and was betrothed to a man she hadn't met. But Arabic women, like women around the world, are not easily controlled.

Ahlam wanted to become a journalist and write about the picturesque world she lived in. Somehow she managed to do that. She attended college where she trained in the art of writing, and she wrote for as many publications as would print her work, sometimes reporting, sometimes creating stories. She fell in love — with a handsome college boy. To survive, she married her betrothed, but kept the handsome college boy in her heart, next to her joy of writing.

Neither Ahlam nor her country, it could be said, have survived. Except that the country of Iraq remains on maps, devastated, still holding onto hope for survival. What will not survive are the remnants of the beginning of time that have been destroyed by the bombs. What will not survive are the memories for ensuing generations of the bounty and charm of the old Iraq, the country that Ahlam and her family knew and loved.

Ahlam's Stories are about that old Iraq, the one her father and grandfather told her about. Her stories recount the way her grandparents met, fell in love, and married. Her stories describe the customs of a society that survived many controlling political powers, including the tyrant that Ahlam knew. Her stories portray the love of parents for their children, especially of women who must witness their children drawn into lives of violence, hate, and prison. And her stories tell about the deaths of those who got in the way.

While it may sound like a story of death and dying — of both Iraq and its people — *Ahlam's Stories* tell about those who survive. Her own survival lay in a flight to safety in another country where she could write her stories. She wanted them to be read by Iraqi youth who never knew Iraq the way it used to be. Stories of those left behind remain to be told, perhaps by other young Iraqi girls, perhaps after studying at college and, perhaps, living in a free and peaceful Iraq that rebuilds its roads, houses, tall buildings, and parks that border the beautiful Tigris.

Both Ahlam and Bmae died on the same day. Neither woman knew of the other, although they lived just a few hundred miles apart — in the Pacific Northwest. Both women had completed writing their stories and were rewriting them to make them "just right".

In retrospect, it seems that both women ran out of steam. Both suffered the kind of illness that invades a body and destroys it slowly. They had fought their fights bravely and so actively that they simply ran out of energy.

Both rushed to complete their stories, at the toll of their physical health. Both women wanted — so very much — to tell their stories. That's all. They wanted to tell their stories. For, if they didn't, who would?

It would seem that I am the survivor. I am the one who must see that the stories of these women are told. Their stories of survival mirror the stories that change lives, inspire another, save lives, encourage others.

Ahlam's Stories is published as an eBook, making it accessible to the numberless young people who have left Iraq, not knowing what their country looked like before....

Bmae's story, *Still the Tall Fir Grows*, is published as both paperback and eBook. These women wrote their first book-length manuscripts, and finished them. That's all a writer wants to know: their work survives.

DANCING WOMEN

Who are these women?

What are their names?

What do they do?

All you have to do is look at them — closely — to see they are the ancients, perhaps the first women on earth. They cluster, not for security, but because they feel each other's strengths and share them. They touch lightly. They smile for the gods who watch. They look into the world. They dance.

What are your names, great Earth Mothers? How are you called?

"Eve."

"My name is Eve."

"My name too is Eve."

"And I also am Eve."

How am I to tell you apart?

"Can you not see us? We are all different. We are called the same, but anyone can see that we are different."

Yes, yes, I can see you are different. Your shapes are slightly different... and...

"No. Our shapes are the same — one head each, two arms, two legs (although they are covered by our skirts). We each have a pair of eyes to see the sky, ears to hear the angels, a nose to catch the waft of wind, hands to touch, and a mouth to voice our innermost expressions. Please don't identify us by shapes. We are human goddesses."

Of course. Yet, each of you has a different appearance.

"Ah, appearance. That is a different matter. Can you tell by our *appearance* how we are different?"

Possibly. Let me look closer. Well, you seem to hold yourself outward. Does that make sense? You seem to be reaching out with those loving hands to connect with others. Hands, I sense without touching, that are warm... and soft... yet strong. You are Caring. Yes, Caring Eve.

"Very good. You have seen with eyes... have you noticed?... that are very like mine."

And you, you who hold your head high, your shoulders straight, your firm arms guiding the dance. I know your body holds the mysteries of new life and that you revel in keeping it ready to do its work. You are physical, you are Healthy Eve.

"Perceptive again. My body expresses our health, yours and mine, our potential to carry and bring forth life."

Ummm, you on the right with your beautifully cut dress, do I see the shape of a heart in your gown? Your smile tells me you love easily. You are caring and sensuous at the same time. Your heart leads you; therefore you must be Heartfelt Eve.

"Right on, sister. You have learned that my heart is as big as yours. We both give love without counting, just as we seek as much love as we give."

You, who dance with eyes staring into the universe, you must then be.... You are the spirit, the ethereal, the dream, the yearning that carries you into the life mist. You are the ongoing stream that transports your genes to mine, the part of first life that I still hold within me. You, my predecessor, my divine ancestor, are Soul Eve.

"How'd she see into us so easily, sisters?"

"She has your hands..."

"Your heart..."

"Your body..."

"And your soul.... Have you noticed her eyes?"

My eyes?

"Yes, you have the eyes of our fifth sister, the one for whom we dance. She has been imprisoned for a long long time, but is now being set free. I'm sure you would recognize her because you are so much like her. She wonders and prods and asks. She knows when to go and when to stay, when to run and when to walk, when to act and when to sit silently, when to speak out and when to be still... as do you."

I'm sure I would recognize her immediately. Does she look deeply into the world's eyes without blinking? Does she command respect with the knowledge that she freely shares? I know she understands that patience and respect are her strengths. Her name is Wisdom Eve. And now, you say, she is free of the bonds that have held her captive for such a long time.

"We dance for her and for us and for you, sweet child of us all. We dance for all women who walk through life as you do — caring and strong and loving and wise, following their souls."

Celebrate, women. Celebrate women. Celebrate and dance.

SECTION II

STORIES AND MORE STORIES

A SQUIRREL'S PAIN

Have you ever heard a squirrel cry? I'm serious! I'm listening to that strange sound now, as I write — a sad ongoing set of loud chattering clacks, one after another after another.

This morning, when I went out to pick up the newspaper, I was surprised to see one of my backyard squirrels near the street at the end of the sidewalk. They seldom come to the front of the house because of the traffic. This one was agitated, pacing and jumping about on the edge of the lawn. When it saw me, the creature hesitated a moment, not wanting to abandon its vigil. Reluctantly, it raced to the safety of a nearby fir tree. There it sat, twitching its tail, waving it about furiously. And, I swear, a look of terror covered its pointy little face.

Then I saw it — another squirrel, or rather its body, lying in the middle of the street. The accident must have happened recently; the body lay crumpled up, unmoving, but not squashed. The next few cars racing past changed that.

I sent my message of condolence to the animal as it cowered amid the tree branches. "I'm so sorry you lost your friend… mate… child…." I waited a few moments, then sent another message, "Please don't go into the street too!"

The chill of the morning sent me back into the house where I continued to check on my friend periodically from the window. The pathetic little squirrel stayed in the tree for a very long time. And my attention turned to the morning chores.

A few hours later, I sat near the back door, reading. This is the place where I often watch visiting squirrels and blue jays enjoy my backyard. Over the years, I've learned to identify them as they steal my tulip bulbs, bury their treasures, munch on the daffodil bulbs, spread crocuses about the yard, and occasionally scold off a marauding cat.

I meet the new squirrel offspring each year. One year I was delighted to watch five little ones on their first outing as they scurried about my lawn during family playtime. I remember the day I watched one of the older squirrels stretch out on the deck railing to sneak an uninterrupted nap in the sun. Its feet straddled the rail and, as I watched, its eyes slowly closed and — I swear — it began to snore.

The sound that catches my attention is different — that strange chattering, loud and constant, that seems to come from the depths of one of the tall pines. It isn't a blackbird (that often causes a ruckus); the sound doesn't fly away.

I quietly walk outside again and lean on the railing that faces the tree. I cannot see it, but I know instantly it is the squirrel, probably sitting near or in its invisible nest. The sound is easy to discern as the grief-stricken wail of a lonely soul that is lost in the survival of a tragedy.

The sad crying continues, soon joined by a strange addition to the cacophony. Similar sounds are coming from distant trees, in all directions. The squirrel community is expressing its grief with my squirrel friend. Even a couple of blackbirds caw their sympathetic cries.

My backyard soon grows silent. And, as I marvel at the response of wild creatures to a friend in pain, I marvel at my own notice of this strange and wonderful phenomenon. Never mind that I don't speak "squirrel", nor do they speak "human". We still can feel pain and empathize with the heartbreak of each other.

FLOODED MEMORIES

Diantha Taylor Lewis sat rocking in the glass-enclosed sunroom of Meadowcrest Resident for the Aged, her eyes taking in the beauty of the scarlet and gold foliage in the park outside, and her bones soaking in the warmth of the sun's rays coupled with the crackling fireplace. She often enjoyed the afternoon sun this way. What else was there to do in a place like this?

She turned as a young woman sat down beside her and asked how she was feeling.

"Fine," she answered.

"Just fine?" the young woman asked.

"Yup. Just fine."

"Did you write down the things I asked the last time I was here?"

"Yes… and no. That wasn't as easy as it sounded."

"I only asked you to write down the highlights of your life, you know, the events and times that you remember, the moments that may have changed your life…"

"You mean, you wanted me to write an autobiography."

"Not exactly. My idea was to get your little gray cells working, you know, like Christie's Hercule Poirot."

"My little gray cells are dying. I know that. Don't fool around with me." The older woman rocked faster, her hands flapping in her lap. Anyone could see she was becoming upset.

"Were you unable to remember?"

"Oh no, my dear. Quite the opposite." The older woman became more agitated.

"What do you mean?"

"It wasn't that I couldn't remember; it was that I couldn't forget." She paused before adding, "And I didn't think anyone would believe me anyway."

"I know you've lived a long time. You must've had some extraordinary moments. Everyone does. I just thought…"

"Well, I'm not sure what you thought, but I am sure *you* won't believe me either." The woman put her hand into her pocket and slowly withdrew a piece of paper. She handed it to the younger woman, who began to read:

Once upon a time…

Gee it's hard to write a story when you realize your whole flaming life has been a lie.

For starters, who would believe that this great intellectual, over-achiever, business dynamo was kicked out of one college and flunked out of graduate school?

Who would believe that my body passed through the eye of a hurricane — a real one — and that my knees felt numb and that I smelled a faint odor of sulfur and nitrogen which made the air feel light and clean and that the stars in the sky over the eye seemed like ceiling lights and that the winds before and after shook the cement walls of the house? Who would believe that?

I mean, how could I ever convince anyone that as a teenager I sang a song about meeting a handsome stranger who would sweep me off my feet and then, less than a decade later, actually met such a man who loved me as much as I loved him. Who would believe that I walked out of his life when a career beckoned.

And who would believe I sat six feet from a President in a press conference in Washington DC, and that I wore a red hat and carried red gloves so he'd notice me? He did.

How could I ever explain the ecstasy of feeling a baby within me for a few weeks, then endure the horror of seeing it flow away in a bloody mass?

Who would believe that I witnessed an eruption of a volcano, saw the black plume spew into the sky and spread like a storm cloud over the countryside, spreading a fine white silt over the green trees and grass until the earth was covered with the sabulous dust of sandpaper?

How could anyone believe I would be awash in money and glory one day and, within months, be faced with eviction, debtor claims, the shame of trying to live without money?

Who would believe I would live through the rainstorms that melted the snow that raised the river that flooded my home and carried off my memories along with the mud, and that for years I would find dried mud in strange places among the few treasures I managed to retrieve?

Who would believe that I have stood atop some of the tallest mountains in the world and felt the joy of watching mere mortals skittering about in the heat miles and miles below, not realizing that I was standing in the snow above their heads waving at them?

How could the princess have so many friends, admirers, well-wishers one moment and the next find they all had disappeared without so much as a goodbye? They never really knew me.

The younger woman re-read the last line slowly, sat back, and covered her eyes with her free hand. The two sat silently for several minutes before the younger woman reached out and clasped the hand of the older woman. After several more moments, she said, "You're right, Mom. I guess I never knew you. But I believe what you wrote… what you lived. You must have had… no, you *did* live a very fascinating life. Somehow I always thought of you beginning life when I did."

"In a way, it did, Sweetie. Bringing a beautiful soul like you into the world was probably the part I remember the best."

Booties

Lena carefully selected a ball of pale yellow yarn, lemon-color, by-passing the pastel pink and blue yarns she kept in her Bootie Knitting Box. "This will make a lovely pair of booties for Clarice's baby." Clarice was waiting for its birth to learn the child's sex. Yellow seemed neutral.

Lena, the family knitter, made sweaters for all the children — her nieces and nephews — and booties for every woman who announced she was pregnant. There were so many lately. Lena's peers all seemed to have waited until their mid-thirties to conceive children.

Familiarity with the bags of yarn in Lena's closet calmed her tensions at the end of a hard day of teaching. Her entire life seemed surrounded by children — the children at school, the neighborhood children who crowded into her kitchen on Saturdays to taste cookies, the children of her two sisters and brother, those being born to her friends who not so long ago were children themselves.

Lena had knit dozens of pairs of booties, in all colors, but mostly in pink and blue. She had bagfuls of them in the closet. Still, when she heard of a new baby on the way, she went to the yarn box, not the bootie bag.

"Yes, yellow is perfect. It feels cool, like lemonade, and will be easy to work with in this hot weather." Lena looped a corner of the yarn around the small needle, settled back in her swivel chair and began to cast on stitches. "One, two, three…" the counting took over and she closed her eyes.

"How can you knit in the dark?" her best friend Emily had asked. The girls, then fourteen, were seated in the movie theater on a Sunday afternoon. Emily opened the bag of popcorn and Lena pulled out her knitting.

"It's easy. I just feel the stitches."

"But what if you miss one?"

"I don't."

"But what if you did…"

"Shhh, Emily, the movie is starting." Lena loved the soft click of the needles and the feel of the yarn slipping along her fingers as she worked on a new sweater. She had been knitting for over a year, and had finished a scarf for her mother, a vest for her sister Alma, and a set of golf covers for her dad. Now it was time to begin a sweater for herself.

Twenty years later, Lena's closet was filled with hand-knit sweaters. And her friends were beginning to benefit from her love of knitting baby booties. "There's something about knitting these little things that I love," she had told her sister.

"You always had a thing for boots," Alma had replied.

"Boots?"

"Yes, boots. Why the funny look on your face?"

"I don't know. When you said that, something flickered through my head, sort of…" Lena stopped, closed her eyes and tried to remember that something.

"You're scaring me, Lena," Alma's voice shook as she reached for her sister's arm.

"It's… it's… okay. Just… something…"

Bang, bang, bang, came the sound of pounding on the door. Then the crashing of wood and hinges and thumping of boots across the hardwood floor. Boom, boom, boom! Furniture tossed, thunder roared, an electric light fixture flared; the pounding continued as the boots marched through hallway, bedrooms, back to the living room.

Lena sat up in her chair, the yellow yarn falling to the floor. Her head hurt from the pounding. What was it? Where did the sound come from?

Teaching during the next few days turned into a chore, unusual for Lena who loved to see children's faces light up. Now their faces remained dark, closed. The air was filled with crying. Hildy cut her finger on a corner of the desk; Joel tripped over his shoelaces during recess and bruised his knee; Mandy and Paul duked it out just before the end of the school day and were sent to the principal's office. Lena's head hurt as she packed her briefcase and headed home.

A quick supper, then Lena turned on "Jeopardy!" and pulled out her knitting. She hadn't gotten very far on the first bootie and decided she'd better get moving; the baby shower was just three days away. The needles clicked softly as she mouthed the answers to Jeopardy questions. At the close of the show, she turned off the set and turned on the radio to listen to evening classical music.

A few years ago, Lena had undergone therapy to help her with sleep problems. She had developed nightmares that defied falling asleep easily. Better to stay awake than face those demons. Her therapist had given her several ways to relax her mind before heading to bed.

Now she was remembering them and trying them again, one at a time. Soft music. Pleasurable pastime — knitting. Comfortable chair.

Lena finished the sole of the bootie and was making the crucial turn of the heel when she thought she heard someone at the door. She sat up straight, but didn't move out of her chair. No, it couldn't be happening — again. Again? That means it happened before. What happened before? Her mind churned, trying to remember the sounds, the feelings, the events.

Pounding boots clomping across the floor, chaos, the scream — just one tiny scream — then the silence. What had happened? Was this something from her childhood? Or something from an old movie?

As far as Lena could tell, her childhood had been uneventful. She was born upstate and moved south when she was about five. The following year, she enrolled in school and became a model student. She graduated from high school at seventeen in the same town and moved on to college.

Four years later, she was a full-fledged teacher, certified and in demand from schools throughout the state. Good grades. Good teaching skills. Good reports from instructors. An ideal teacher-candidate, it hadn't been difficult to secure her first job. Now, at 34, she was teaching at her third position, a class of adorable, inquisitive sixth graders who kept her intrigued and on her toes every day.

"What did this idyllic childhood have to do with pounding boots and mayhem?" her therapist had asked. And Lena couldn't answer.

She finally had the courage to ask her sister one day. "Alma, do you remember any violence in our childhood?" Alma was two years older and would certainly know if any such thing had happened.

"Why on earth do you ask?" Alma seemed amazed.

"Do you? Remember anything?"

"No. Of course not. Mommy and Daddy were very much in love. And they loved us very much. I don't remember anything even bordering on loudness, much less violence. What's going on?"

"Apparently I'm having something my therapist calls flashbacks, or shadow memories. She says there's something in there and I can't get it out."

"Certainly not from *our* childhood. Maybe you read something, or saw something in a movie."

"That's what I thought. But lately, it's been happening again. Things are coming to mind that bother me — a lot!"

"What kind of things?"

"Boots."

"Boots? What kind of boots?"

"Heavy, angry, pounding boots. Like someone marching across the floor, pushing stuff out of the way, hurting somebody." Lena cringed at the thought.

"Lena!" Alma wrapped her arms around her sister. "Honey, what a dreadful image!"

"But it's so vivid, Alma. It's so clear. I can see those boots as if... as if..."

"Lena, what's wrong?"

"I'm... not... sure. I just had an image of an animal, of blood, of guns and knives and..."

"Do you remember if Dad ever went hunting?"

"I don't think so. You'd remember better than I."

"I vaguely seem to remember when I was about six — just before we moved away from Chaseville — Dad and his friends had been out with... guns..."

"Guns? Are you sure?"

"Yes, guns. It must have been a hunting trip. They must have gone hunting."

The two girls sat hugging each other, trying to search their memories for clues, details of a time long ago when their minds recorded images easier than they recorded words. Nothing surfaced.

That evening Lena sat with her knitting and carefully finished the sock part of the bootie, adding pique loops around the top. When she finished, she snipped off the yarn and held it up. "There, perfect. Now for the other foot."

As she prepared the loop for the second bootie, loud pounding boots clattered across the floorboards, moving swiftly from the front door to the back room where she sat. Big black boots that came just to the eye level of a small child. Big black boots that stomped around the room, dislodging furniture and tossing about items that weren't fastened down. A scream from the bedroom and Lena jumped from her chair. "Mama, I'm here," she called. Yet she knew her mother had been gone for many years.

"Lena," came the shrill voice. "Lena!"

"Mama? Where are you?"

"Lena, call your father."

"Where is he?"

"I don't know. Call him."

"Mama!"

But the silence that followed came too quickly. The boots disappeared. Mama disappeared. The silence disappeared too, in time.

Still, the images lingered in the child's head. The images of boots, of panic, of silence.

Saturday Knight

When Saturday Knight was in a room, everyone knew it. That is, if she wanted them to know. If she was on a case, she could make herself quite invisible.

Like now. If I didn't tell you, you'd never recognize her. See? Over there? Next to the louvered window? She's the old woman leaning against the wall, the one with the scarf on her head.

Saturday wears the scarf when she's in a hurry — to cover her hair. Oh, that flaming head of bright orange hair. You can't mistake her for anyone else. The long curly locks that frame an angelic face with her sparkling brown eyes and classic cheekbones should be enough to notice, but add the walk, the way she holds her shoulders back, her head high, and lets her long legs carry her through a door, across a carpet, down an arched hallway. She says it's her goddess impression. I think she does it on purpose.

During the times she wants everyone to know she's in the room, she draws the attention she needs to fuel her high energy spirit. If she doesn't want to be seen, you can bet she won't.

Watch her. She's impersonating an old woman. She walks slowly, stooped over a bit to avoid looking directly at people. It wouldn't matter, since nobody notices old women anyway. And that's what makes Saturday great at her work. She's a P.I. — private investigator. She often has to follow people without them knowing it.

I think it was her grandmother, Merry Knight, who gave her the tip. You know, that business about old women being invisible.

Merry used to tell her granddaughter how she enjoyed taking Saturday with her when she wanted to get things done. People paid attention to the little girl with the mop of orange hair. Then Gran could slip in her request or her question and get action. Like the time she went to the Social Security office and took Saturday along. That was the first time she didn't have to wait. The man at the door took one look at the smiling child and ushered her (and her grandmother) into a cubicle.

At first Gran thought it was a fluke, a coincidence. But Saturday was with her the time she returned a pair of shoes to the department store. "Yes, Ms. Knight. Of course, Ms. Knight. We'll replace them immediately, Ms. Knight," said the clerk without taking her eyes off the young Saturday.

"Aha!" thought Ms. Knight. "She's the reason I'm getting such immediate service." To prove it, she returned to the shoe department the next day, talked to the exact same clerk, and realized the clerk had never seen her before. "Aha! That's all the proof I need."

After that, whenever Merry Knight wanted to get things done, she took Saturday with her. As her granddaughter grew older, Merry explained why she often insisted that Saturday accompany her to places that weren't exactly designed for young girls.

Saturday got a kick out of watching the way people reacted to her. And she also noticed the way they didn't react to her grandmother. This was Saturday's education in the ways of the world, and she couldn't thank her grandmother enough for the insight.

When Saturday opened her investigative business, she used this bit of information to advantage. She picked up a gray wig, a plain dress and coat, and what she called *old lady shoes* at a thrift store.

"That's what they mean by plain clothes," she murmured as she gazed at the mirror. The wig covered her hair; the clothes played down her long legs; and if she wore glasses or kept her gaze toward the floor, her bright eyes didn't explode on her face. "I'm not sure I'd pay any attention to me either."

Oh-oh. Something's happening. Watch Saturday as she walks up to the counter and waits for a clerk. She's standing next to one, but the man seems to be looking past her — toward the couple that just walked up. Sure enough. The clerk is talking to the couple. Saturday waits.

"We're checking out," the woman speaks abruptly to the desk clerk. "We've changed our minds about staying tonight." The clerk begins to scan his computer.

"Was there anything wrong with the room?" he asks.

"No," the woman answers curtly. "We're just leaving."

"Come one," her partner urges. "I'm getting antsy."

"Shhh. Keep calm," the woman whispers. Saturday moves closer. No one pays any attention to her.

"I can't help it. You heard Jake. He'd said he was sending someone right over. Let's just go."

"Do you want the hotel to send someone after us? Just stay calm. We have time." To the clerk, she adds, "We're in a bit of a rush. Can you give us our bill please?"

"I'm totaling up your room service checks now," the clerk responds lazily, unconcerned about their haste.

The woman calmly takes her partner's arm and begins to stroke it. "Nice and quiet, dear. Just stay nice and quiet." But the man is becoming more anxious.

"I can't. If they go into that room before we're out of here…"

"They won't. Housekeeping won't go in until we're checked out."

"But if they do…"

"Oh, for heaven's sake, Will. You're such a pain. Jake and his boys are on the other side of town. You know they won't call the cops. They're in this as much as we are. Now just think pleasant thoughts. Rio in January. Warm sunshine. All that money in our names. And nobody at Baily-Watts any the wiser."

Saturday moves away from the couple, shuffles around the corner and pulls out her cell phone. She dials and waits. "Lieutenant Meyer. Saturday Knight. I have your perps, the ones who pulled off the extortion at the Baily-Watts Company. They're at the checkout desk of the Hamilton Plaza Hotel. Do you want me to intercept or can you get somebody over here within five minutes?" She listens, then returns, "Okay. You're the boss. I'll wait, but only until they start to move."

She closes the phone and pockets it, turning just enough to watch the desk clerk as he grinds out duplicate copies of the bill for the woman to sign. She doesn't have five minutes.

"Excuse me," she pushes her way toward the clerk. "Excuse me. I've been waiting here and I need to talk to you right away." The clerk barely notices. Saturday repeats her request, moving closer to the couple.

"I'll be right with you," the clerk responds dully, not looking at her.

"No, right now. I've waited long enough. I wish to place a complaint about my room. The people in the next room were up all night talking and banging around their room. I couldn't sleep at all…"

Saturday talks as fast as she can, drawing out her story longer and longer, keeping the clerk tied up. The woman customer stands gaping at her, pen suspended in mid-air.

Both she and the man seem to forget momentarily they are in a hurry. They're still standing there gaping at that foolish old woman, listening to her strange story of discomfort, when Lt. Meyer and his squad stride into the lobby.

As fast as the cuffs are placed on the couple, the old woman disappears. Saturday dashes to her car and heads back to the office, the tape of the conversation still throbbing under her coat. She reaches in, holds the microphone for a moment as she inserts the time and place, then guns the engine of her turquoise Mustang as she triumphantly calls out, "Case Closed."

THE COMPANION

Camilla was not an attractive woman. She wasn't ugly, she just didn't dress herself up or use makeup. She was a tall woman, much like you might imagine a Nebraska pioneer farm woman to be, with thick waist, muscular arms, and a strong back. Janice regarded her as a godsend when she entered her mother's life... at first.

"Your ad said you wanted a companion for your mother," Camilla said, holding out the newspaper clipping.

"That's right. Mother wants to live by herself, away from family. We feel she needs a companion to drive her places, spend time with her, remind her of her medicine. Do you have a family?"

"Just a sister... in North Dakota. No, I'm alone. I'm a professional companion. I have cared for other women, and I have references. It's what I do. I enjoy being a companion to someone who needs me. Will I have a private room?" Camilla asked.

"Of course. We'll expect you to live at her house and be available to her at all times. You'll have two half-days and a full day off each week. I work at the office and can take work home when it's necessary. We'll work out a schedule."

Camilla accepted the terms. A lonely woman, she seemed happy to have a place to stay. And Janice's mother was a pleasant woman to care for. She loved to joke and play games, even if she didn't remember the scores, and sometimes, even the game.

She wasn't always like that, Janice remembered. There had been times when Mother managed her husband's business, keeping a shop full of workers producing high quality shoes for men. Janice's dad had died when she was a teenager and she had been surprised at the way her mother took over the business. But her mother had aged, and Janice had taken over her job.

After the companion was hired, Janice returned to work, assured that Camilla would take good care of Mother. When Janice took her mother to her own home during Camilla's time off, the older woman seemed happy. At first. It was after about a year with Camilla that Janice began to notice changes in her mother.

About two months earlier, Janice thought her mother's mind was drifting during their conversations. The doctors had said that the medication she was taking should keep her in the present, lucid, aware of her surroundings. Maybe it was just age, but Janice felt she was losing her self-assured mother and gaining a senile old woman.

"Mother, where are you?" Janice tested. "Mother, who am I?"

"Ask Camilla," the old woman responded sharply.

"What do you mean? Don't you know where you are?"

"Of course. But I have to ask Camilla if it's all right to tell you."

"Mother. I'm your daughter. Camilla's not here. Of course you can talk to me."

"Okay. Where is Camilla?" The old woman's eyes appeared glazed as she searched the room for her companion. "Did she leave me? She said she would."

"No, she's just taking a day off. She'll be back this evening." Janice noticed her mother's neck tense at the words. After a moment, she asked, "Don't you want her to come back?"

"Yes. No. Yes. Will she?"

"Mother, what's going on? What is happening between you and Camilla?"

"I can't say. Not unless Camilla says so."

Janice changed her questioning. "Mom, where have you and Camilla been going to eat out?"

"I don't know."

"You mean you can't remember?"

"No, I don't know. She drives me places and I'm not sure where we are. I just go with her."

"What do you do when you're home in the evening? Do you still enjoy Scrabble?"

"Sometimes we play games. Mostly I watch television while she does her work."

"What work?"

"Her project, she calls it. I don't know what it is." Again, the old woman searched the room looking for her companion.

Janice tried another approach. "What would you like for lunch today? We could have soup with crackers or a sandwich? Peanut butter? Chicken salad? Or would you rather have some cottage cheese? I know you like that."

"You decide," her mother said dully.

"No, Mother. I want you to choose."

"Anything is all right with me."

"Mother. I want you to choose your lunch. Tell me what you want to eat." Janice's voice had taken on an edge as she began to sense an eerie logic behind her mother's change. "You decide, Mom."

The old woman's lips pushed against each other and her eyes blinked to hold back the tears. As she closed her eyes, a few tears spread onto her cheeks, exposing a woman who was suffering. "I… I…" she spoke slowly, painfully. "I… can't."

Janice moved to take her mother's arm and gently caressed the old woman's face. "What's wrong, Mommy?" she whispered.

"I can't… I can't… I can't make choices," she began. "I can't decide anything anymore. I try to ask for what I want, but Camilla doesn't hear." Her anger rising, she was close to yelling and paused to take in air, grabbing bits of it in gulps, one after another, like a child in pain.

"She just takes me where she wants to go, feeds me what she wants to eat, plays what she wants to play, talks about what she wants…" she sobbed, her pain turning to rage. "She won't let me do anything I want to. She tells me when to get up, when to go to bed…"

The woman struck her daughter with her fist to accent her words. Janice held her mother until the fury was spent.

"I love you, Mom. I'm glad you told me about this. I'm sorry if you aren't getting along with Camilla, but she's the only way I can be sure you're taken care of."

The old woman whimpered in reply.

"I wish I could do something more, but you'll have to get used to her ways. Maybe she's bossy, maybe even pushy, but you know I can't take care of you here. Not like you need caring for. You're going to have to get used to..."

"I don't want to get used to her," the old woman cried.

"But Mom, Camilla is a professional. She knows how to be a companion."

Janice's mother slumped in her chair. Her fight had been fought and she had no more energy. She watched her daughter spread peanut butter on a piece of bread and thought, "I don't know which one I hate more — my companion or my daughter."

STOLEN NOTHING

Once upon a time there lived a thief. As a child, she took small things, and as she grew, her thefts also grew.

By the time she was a tall child, she knew how to take just about any item she wanted, and soon became bored with the simplicity of thieving.

"How can I stay interested in the world?" she asked herself. Soon the answer came. "I'll learn to take that which cannot be seen."

Soon, she achieved her goal. She was stealing patience, trust, responsibility, cooperation, honesty, and love. The theft of love most intrigued her and satisfied her needs.

"How do you steal love?" you ask. And it's good to ask.

First she stole all the other parts from others: her parents, her sister and brother, and their friends (for she had none of her own). She eventually stole their love.

And then came the surprise, and probably her greatest achievement in thievery. She stole the love of a stranger.

Delighted with herself, she soon learned to steal love from anyone, everyone until her pastime became obsession. She soon needed to have it all… all the love in the world.

Until one day she had it all. She had stolen love from everyone. "I have all the love in the world," she bragged.

But the joke was on her. When she tried to enjoy what she had stolen, she realized she could see none of it. She had nothing to show for all her work.

Because she had nothing to begin with, no love for herself.

TOMMY, TOMMY, TOMMY, TOMMY, WHOOPS, TOMMY

Tommy's a fuck-up! I'm doing it again, fucking up my whole damn life. Tommy, Tommy, Tommy, Tommy, Whoops, Tommy… why the hell am I thinking of that kids' game tonight? God, I can see Mom's face as she played that old trick on me. I must have been two, no three or four. She'd hold up her hand and tell me to copy exactly what she did. Then she'd count her fingers, from pinky to pointer, saying "Tommy, Tommy, Tommy, Tommy." Then she'd slide her finger between her pointer and thumb, saying, "Whoops," and end up pointing to her thumb.

"Tommy, now you do it — exactly as I did," she'd say. I'd repeat the process, trying so hard to get it right, repeating exactly what she did, but at the end she'd always say, "No, that isn't exactly right. Watch me closely." Then she'd repeat the whole thing. And I'd try again and again and again. It seemed that even back then I couldn't get things right. So I guess you could say I was fucking up at the age of two, or three or four.

And I guess I've done it again tonight. I shouldn't have had so much to drink. But it's spring and, hell, we were celebrating the rites of spring, new life, new hope... hope... hope... hope I get home tonight down this damn mountain road. Whoa, take it easy, Tommy, that was a patch of ice, and that shoulder leads down the side of the mountain, a long way down. Down. Slow down. Yeah, slow down.

Mom used to say that as she tried to show me what I was doing wrong. "Slow down and watch carefully. Tommy, Tommy, Tommy, Tommy, Whoops, Tommy. Now you do it — right this time." And I kept falling for it. Even after I knew the secret.

I fell for it again, when I was ten, because I had forgotten. But I got back because I was old enough then to try it on somebody else, my little brother and sister and my big brothers' unsuspecting friends. There were always kids around our house to play tricks on. With three brothers and two sisters, there were always kids around, some more gullible than the rest.

Hey, I just realized I'm a middle kid. Aren't middle kids always fucked up? Actually both my sister and I are middle kids. Kimmy, dear sweet Kim. I wonder if she's as fucked up as I am. She doesn't seem to be now, but she was a few years ago when she first brought Carlos home. We thought he was a monster who had hypnotized her, like Shaw's "Pygmalion". Kimmy was still in school and he was older, two, maybe three years older, and he had his own truck and he lived away from his folks. "He must be magic," Mom concluded. Then he stole her away from Mom and she was furious, but Kim was happy. God, she was... is... happy with Carlos. We were all so wrong. Why can't they see how happy Kim is with Carlos?

Why couldn't they see how happy I was with Ann? Why couldn't they see that Ann was the best thing that ever happened to me? Ann... Ann. I can see your face as clear as if you were sitting next to me in this truck. Are you here? Really here? I feel like you are. Or is it the beer? Ann, we could have gone through with it, had the kid. I'd have married you and we could have lived happily ever after.

Whoops, Tommy, you screwed that one up too. Just like you screwed up everything from the very beginning.

When did you start screwing up, really? High school? No, before that. Dropping out of high school was the tail of major screw-ups that began long before, way back in... must have been first grade. Yeah, you never could learn the Tommy, Whoops, Tommy trick, even in school.

The only good thing about school was the drawing. That was the only time I could do anything the way I wanted. I had so looked forward to taking music classes too. Didn't I already know how to play my guitar and Mom's piano? But old Mr. What's-his-name insisted I learn trumpet. They needed trumpets, fucking trumpets. Who the hell wants to play a trumpet?

School! *Tommy, you have to learn to sit in your seat when you're in class. Tommy, you can go out in the schoolyard at recess and run and play. But now, Tommy, you sit still.* God, I hate to sit still. I hated it then and I hate it now. "Sit still, Tommy." Hell no... HELL NO! I won't sit still. No more, not for anybody.

Jeez, there's another patch of ice… better slow down, not so fast, Tommy.

Then they wanted me to read all that history stuff all over. Hell, I've read more history than was in their books, and all they wanted me to do was repeat the stuff they made me read the year before.

High school was a bore. I remember how much I looked forward to going to high school, following my big brothers up the ladder, maybe playing baseball with them. I could play with them for just a year before Mike graduated. Too late for playing with Steve; he was already out, working, and married. We played together enough in the backyard anyway. That was one good thing about having brothers, somebody to play with — baseball, football, music.

Yes, the music, that was the best part, Mom or Kim at the piano, Steve and me with our guitars, Mike on drums. Jeannie never learned to play. Kevin wasn't playing yet, but he was learning. Little Kev was too busy holding down jobs at fast food chains. Damn he was industrious. Why couldn't I be more industrious? Mom wants to know: Why can't Tommy with all his brains and talent get a job? Didn't I stick out a whole summer laying concrete with Steve? DIDN'T I SWEAT ENOUGH FOR YOU, MOM?

That was the year I was sixteen, god, nearly ten years ago… no nine. That last birthday was my twenty-fifth. Can you believe it? Twenty-five years old and still fucking up. Steve was married twice by the time he was twenty-five. Mike had a good old job with Dad when he was twenty-five.

Here I am, still fucking up like I did that year I was sixteen. Back to school? No way! By the second day, I could see the writing on the wall? No, they weren't assignments, fuckhead; they were words to predict the future. Ha! BORING, ENDLESS HASSLES, NO WAY! I skipped. I ran.

That was the year I went to California and played with the jazz band before I got too far into the drugs. That was the year I found love for the first time, Betsy, was that her name? I remember her soft blond hair kept getting in my eyes. God, she was beautiful, but... isn't there always a *but*?

How many others were there before Ann? What fucking way could I ever be able to count, always unconscious, numb from the stuff I was swallowing. How can a kid of seventeen be so dead to life? It was all around me and I chose to be dead to it. Does that sound like a bright boy? Does that sound right, man? No way. No way.

Jeez, I was glad when I ODed and Mom came to bail me out again. How she hated seeing me handcuffed to that hospital bed. Yeah, I remember how she cried and told me there wasn't anything I could do so wrong she wouldn't love me.

But then she started hitting me with the words again. "Dumb, stupid, wrong, get your act together, kid, you're almost twenty."

I wanted to. I wanted to so much, I even fell for that rehabilitation jazz. Was that the fancy one with the crazy purple window blinds? Or was that the camp? No, the camp came later. The camp was only two years ago, after Mom said she was really giving up on me, giving me another *one last chance*. That was when she sent me to camp!

Yeah, I remember. I had really fucked up that time, set somebody's house on fire. They were going to put me away as an arsonist or some goddamn thing, but Mom and her lawyer got them to put me away in that goddamn camp. Cutting trees in the middle of some goddamn forest, a million miles from nowhere.

Well, I got out of that one too, didn't I? Damn near killed myself doing it, but staying there would have killed me just as fast. One fucking long walk, but how beautiful it was — silent, peaceful, with that goddamn blue sky holding down those towering green spindly trees while the golden aspens beneath rustled ever so softly in the autumn breeze.

God, Tom, you're spouting poetry again. Nobody ever liked your poetry... but Mom... and Ann. Ann, she was at the end of that long walk out of those mountains. Ann, with her bright blue cat's eyes and her straight black hair.

I teased her about being a Native American with blue eyes, and she told me she was, partly. Ann with her long sighs, her deep yoga breathing, her strong hands, her soft body. Ann with her tears, watered by those bluish eyes, her arms holding me, long after we made love, her face sleeping next to mine... Ann...

Damn, more ice! Damn mountain road!

Where's the fucking moon? It was out a few minutes ago, helped light this damn road, made the trees stand out against the night sky, or is it morning? Whoa, Tommy, you'll get home before it's light; just take it easy.

Yeah, I screwed up with Ann, just like everything else. What ever made me think I could straighten out for her, with her? What ever made us think we could have a life together? The baby? Maybe that was our way of telling us to try, but then Mom came in and yelled so loud. The only choice, she told me, was to get rid of the baby and decide if Ann and I had a life together before starting another one.

"That's your only choice!" She said it like that — loud. And I believed her. Was that your trick, Mom? Was that the Whoops, Tommy trick? I remember now, the way you so smugly folded your hands at the end of the game, waiting for me to catch on. That was the trick. You didn't think I'd catch on! But the trick was on you, Mom, because I remembered from watching you play your damn game with the other kids. The trick was in the folding of your hands at the end. But I knew that if I folded my hands, the game was over, and you'd go away, back to your kitchen or your bedroom. You'd go away if I folded my hands, so I spent my whole fucking life trying to keep the game going, trying not to fold my hands and end it. Playing your game to keep you there, talking to me, holding me, loving me.

But the game always ends, and as hard as I tried, I couldn't hold onto you. Let's play once more, Mom, and this time I'll fold my hands. Tommy, Tommy, Tommy, Tommy, Whoops, Tommy, one last fuck-up, faster now, hard on the accelerator, steer straight, don't follow the curve, straight over the top of the trees… look, Mom, I'm folding my hands.

A Shot Rang Out…

Our group is sitting in the coffee shop on Broadway, the doors wide open on a sunny spring day. A shot rings out. We all hear it, clearly a gunshot.

"That was close, maybe over there," one of my friends says as she points to the building across the street.

"That building?" another asks. Nobody moves.

We watch.

Within seconds, a young woman wearing an expensive lightweight coat, gloves, and high heels, runs out of the building carrying a small object in her hand. Her shoulder purse flies loosely behind her. She slows herself, takes aim, and flings the object against the fence directly across the street from where we sit watching. Is it a small gun? She then hurries off, up the hill toward Market Street.

We rush across the street to find the small brown paper bag, neatly folded, with writing on it. No one wants to get close enough to read it. No one wants to touch it. The bag could contain a gun; the writing could be a confession. As we stand there, trying to decide what to do, someone asks, "Has anybody called the cops?"

"Should we?" another replies.

A youngish man, well-dressed in a Madison Avenue suit and hat, comes through the door of the same building. He carries a larger paper bag in his hand, extended away from his body. "Here's the culprit; I bagged him," he says proudly, and deposits the bag in the trash bin.

"A rat?" someone says. "Good old waterfront."

We smile sheepishly and move back to the shop and our coffee. The man gets into his car and drives off.

"A rat," we tell the shopkeeper.

"Did you see it?" a customer asks from a nearby table.

"No. No one actually looked inside the sack."

"What about the smaller bag?" another asks. "Did you ever look at that? What was written on it? What was in it?"

We look at each other.

"You know I'm going back to my apartment to write this, don't you?" I tell them. They nod.

"Could there be a body up there? Still warm? Still breathing?"

"Maybe. Should we get involved?"

THE MUSIC TEACHER

There are no holidays between the Fourth of July and Labor Day — sometimes covering a period of two months. There aren't any holidays in June either — which makes the summer longer, with only one holiday between Memorial Day and the first Monday in September. But it's a boomer!

In the small college town of Avril, the Fourth of July began with a bang at sunup and continued all day and long into the night that followed. Children popped firecrackers and swung sparklers; their dads fired off small bombs that reminded them of the war they had just abandoned. Occasionally a brave mother would light a smoky curly worm or send up a mild Roman candle.

Hannah Mason wondered each year if her child was listening to the great noises. She remembered only the noise now, because her sight had disappeared long ago, just as the child entered her world. Now they both were gone, sight and son. "Son and sun — I can't see either one," she mused. From her vantage point on the porch she could tell just who was shooting off whizzers and who was sending up great splendors that elicited oohs and aahs.

AD MON ISH MENT

As darkness fell, she was joined on the porch by her friend, Calpurnia, the high school girl from next door who took piano lessons from Ms. Mason. She was "Ms." then, in the late 1970s, as were many of the instructors at the college. "Do call me Hannah, Cal," Ms. Mason requested.

"That's okay, Ms. Mason. Your name kinda sings, you know, music..." And Cal stuck with the respectful title.

Today Cal seemed moody. "Something bothering you, Cal?"

"Uh, not exactly, Ms. Mason."

"Are you working on that new Bach sonata?"

"Oh sure. I think I have it now."

"Then it's something else?"

"Well, yeah, I mean…"

"Can I help?"

"No!" The speed and vehemence of Cal's answer surprised Hannah.

"Maybe I can…"

"No. It's nothing. Oh, by the way, the City Opera Company is planning an entire presentation of Verdi next month — to help get us through the dog days of August, I guess."

"Want to go? I have season tickets."

"Sure. Cool." The two women sat in silence, Cal speculating about why Ms. Mason bought two season tickets to the opera each year and Hannah searching for a sense that would explain Cal's strange voice that morning.

"There goes a huge red flare," Cal offered.

"Yes, I heard the fizzing sound. Is it beautiful?"

"Oh my yes. It looks like little tongues of flame. Ooh, and there's a blue shower. That looks like the drops of water to put out the flame."

"My, aren't you poetic," Hannah teased. "Fire and water. Rather like the music, isn't it?"

"You feel the music, don't you?"

"Yes. Maybe it's because I can't see, but the music sinks right into my bones."

Two friends, one older and not-so-much wiser than the other; the other still scratching at the colored stars in her eyes. Throughout the day, neighbors dropped by to greet the music teacher as she sat in the porch swing. "Hi, Hannah," came a voice. "Hi back atcha, Marcella," Hannah would reply. She knew everyone's voice as well as most of them knew their neighbors' faces.

"How do you do that, Ms. Mason?" Cal asked.

"Do what?"

"Recognize people's voices."

"Oh, there's something unique about each voice. A voice is a fingerprint — each one has a special sound, a special quality. You can change the tone, speed, even the accent of words, but you can't alter that basic something. Rather like a soul. You can change what you look like, but you can't change who you are — inside — in your soul."

"I'd like to change me — everything about me," Cal said then, shifting in her wooden porch chair.

"What on earth for?"

"You know, my hair, my face, my body, my… I guess yes, even my soul."

"Calpurnia… what is going on with you today? You aren't suggesting you run away, are you?"

There was a long pause. "Not exactly. Sometimes I wish I could. I'd dye my hair, cut it short, real short, and wear big clothes so I'd look larger, and put on makeup to change my eyes and cheeks and stuff, and…"

"You seem to have thought this out."

"Not exactly. But I have been thinking. The kids at school don't know me. Like you say, my soul, my insides. I don't have any friends who understand about me."

"Is that why you take your music so seriously, Cal? Is that why you work so hard at it?"

"I think music is a way of reaching that deep part inside?"

"It's what keeps me going, makes *me* get up every day. I couldn't live without music."

"Well then, why wouldn't music be a basic part of who I am?"

"Are you saying you'd like to study music professionally?"

"I'm not ready for that yet, but yes… maybe someday."

Another starburst showered the neighborhood with colored light. Cal sighed deeply and Hannah remembered the colors. Why couldn't she reach that level of belief in the power of music? How long had it been since she had felt that power as Cal is feeling it now?

Hannah knew in her heart that something was lacking in her life. Was it Tanya? Was it her husband? Was it… that other one? that long ago nightmare? How can I know the voices of all these people in Avril and not remember the song of my child's voice?

"Goodnight, Cal. Thank you for enjoying the fireworks show with me tonight."

"Goodnight, Ms. Mason. I sure wish you could have seen it."

"Oh I did. Through your eyes. Thank you, my dear."

Small town people become comfortable with their neighbors, until they feel very much like family. And what is family after all if not people living close together? Hannah realized that her family consisted of her neighbors, and her neighbors made up her family.

Which may explain why the entire neighborhood rallied to Hannah's front yard the minute they heard she was missing.

Two days after the Fourth, Hannah's students collected on the porch steps as their appointed practice times came and went. Two, then three, then four youngsters, music books in hand, sat grousing about Miss Hannah. "She's forgotten us," said one.

"No, she's had an ee-mergenc-ee," proclaimed another.

"Maybe she's been kidnapped," suggested a little boy with big eyes behind big glasses.

"Maybe she's sick… or… tied up… or… or lost. She can't see, you know."

By the day's end, police had been notified, the house had been searched, and Ms. Hannah Mason was declared, indeed, to be missing. Her house had been unlocked — everyone's was in this little college town. Police Deputy Arnie Jefferson found no signs of violence, just signs of neatness. "Ain't never seen a house as neat as Miz Hannah's," he told his captain. "It's neat all right. Everything in place and nuthin' needin' dustin'!"

Hannah was neat, if nothing else. She needed things in their place so she could find them easily and not trip over them. As for the dust, she daily drifted through her house with a feather duster, whisking the dust from one place to another, never letting it rest.

"Would she have gone away without canceling her music lessons?" asked the captain.

"Don't think so," was the consensus of neighbors. "She was a stickler for being on time."

"Then where is she? Where did she go?"

"Anybody know anything about her family? Could there have been a family problem?"

"Don't know. She never talks about a family. Never seen any family visitors."

"What about a vacation? Has she talked about taking time off?"

"She said she needed one," spoke up the little boy with the big eyes behind big glasses.

"It was usually at… the end… of… my… lesson," he said, his voice dropping as he realized the sarcasm.

"Deputy Jefferson," the captain announced loudly, "seems we need to call in the experts on this. Could this have been a kidnapping?"

"Well, Captain, if it was, she was kidnapped by someone she knew. There ain't a chair out of place in that house. She went willingly, or at least quietly."

IN VES TI GA TION

Within six hours, the FBI kidnapping team had arrived. Well, not exactly a team, more like two investigators: Jeremy Phillips and Millicent Fennimore. Romy Phillips seemed young, very young for a job like his. Still, he looked the part. Snappy suit, pale blue shirt, and red tie — government uniform. Milly Fennimore, somewhat older, wore a navy suit with skirt, a similar pastel shirt, and a beret. Probably not government issue, but she looked good, and they both appeared to be efficient.

"Where's her purse?" Millicent asked the captain.

"Purse? Didn't see no purse," he answered.

"Hmmm. I don't think this is a crime scene."

"Well, damn, Missus, where the heck is Mrs. Mason?" The captain swore under his breath and waved behind him as he turned over the case to the FBI agents.

The third day after Hannah's disappearance, the investigators were wending their way through the neighborhood. "Tell me about Hannah," was their mantra. Their answers varied like no mantra ever would:

"She's a music teacher. What do you expect? She lived quietly."

"For a long time she has taught my Barbara, even when Barbara doesn't play very well. That Mrs. Mason is a saint. She just kept teaching my Barbara."

"Once, everything mattered to her. She took notice of such details. Then, nothing seemed to matter anymore."

"She used to sing along with my Jenny when she rehearsed her beautiful music, you know, like the wedding songs Jenny sings at weddings and things. She didn't… doesn't sing with her anymore."

"Ms. Mason screamed at me a couple weeks ago, 'If you don't want to improve, don't ask for criticism!' I didn't ask for criticism. I just asked how I sounded."

"Ms. Hannah was always patient… until lately. She grabbed my fingers one day and held 'em so tight I thought they'd break. Then she kinda tossed my hands back at me."

"I challenged her once to listen to her feelings. She said she couldn't hear them. She said, 'Maybe I don't have any'." That was from Cal, the neighbor girl. "That's why I listened to her on the Fourth when she snapped at me because I asked if she was feeling okay. She seemed to be far off in space or something."

"I saw Miss Hannah sitting and crying one day when I got to my lesson. I asked if she felt bad and she just nodded.

I think she was feeling very bad. My lesson that day was very short."

Little by little, the inspectors picked up clues about Hannah Mason, who she was, and how she lived.

No one ever saw her with anyone other than townspeople or her college students. She didn't mix with the faculty — except old Miss Sarah, the chancellor.

Occasionally they had tea at Miss Sarah's office. "She came usually mid-week to sit and chatter about her students," Miss Sarah told Millicent. "We never talked about personal matters. Sometimes she sang." The old woman closed her eyes for a moment. Then, "Oh wait, there was a very strange thing that happened last week."

"What was that?"

"She laid her head back… she was sitting right where you are… and she hummed a bit, then shook her head like she was trying to shake it loose."

"Did she say anything?"

"Yes. After a moment, she said she was trying to remember a song. Some song that seemed important, but she couldn't recall it."

"Uh, oh. Okay, seems we have what we need. Thank you." Millicent stood then, and walked out of the old stone administration building and back to her car. This was a pretty campus, one that would appeal to anyone wanting peace and quiet. But what kind of peace and quiet was Hannah Mason after? She had been here only six years. Where was she before that? Who has she known in her life? Why can't we find any ties to anything or anyone?

"C'mon, Milly, don't let this get to you. I'll bet Ms. Mason will turn up in a few days — just went for a walk, or something as commonly silly."

"You're all heart, Romy. I hope she turns up too, but there are so many questions."

"What do we have? She's a music teacher. She has students who come to learn piano and singing. She lives alone. She's a neatnik. She doesn't receive much mail and never has visitors from 'the outside'. Maybe she's an alien!"

"Romy, now you're being just plain stupid. Listen, why didn't she have visitors? Where is her family? Where are her roots? Surely she grew up somewhere. And why have people noticed a change in her lately?"

"Her music. She must have studied somewhere? Maybe we can check colleges in the state."

"Yeah, and we can run her name through the files. We might get lucky."

"Usually when people are as careful and neat as her, there's something to hide."

"She's blind, you idiot. She has to keep things neat or she'd trip over things."

"Wait, there's another question. How'd she get blind?"

"Yeah, there must be institutions for the blind. Maybe we can check on those."

For two more days, the FBI inspectors wandered about town, haunted the telegraph office, and spent hours on the telephone. Still, they came up empty-handed.

"For cripe's sake, you must have something," yelled their supervisor over the telephone one afternoon in the middle of July. "This woman has to have a past. That's Investigation Procedure 101," he screamed.

Their break occurred near the end of July when the investigators intercepted a letter addressed to Ms. Hannah Mason, Avril College. It was from Bernard Mason and postmarked from a town in the next state. It read simply: *You missed the child support payment this month. Are you in trouble?*

CO NUN DRUM

But it was enough to send Milly and Romy to visit the man. When they knocked on the door, they were greeted by a smallish man of about 45, slightly balding, with a small dark mustache.

"Bernard Mason?"

"Yes. You the FBI?"

"May we come in?"

"You say that Hannah is missing?"

Milly noted that he didn't say, "my wife".

"Since July Fourth. Her neighbors and friends seem concerned. Have you seen her?"

"Not since she left."

"And when was that?"

"Five, no six and a half years ago. Tanya was six; now she's twelve."

"Your daughter?"

"Yes."

"And Hannah's?"

"Yes."

"Do we have the right Hannah?" asked Romy. "About 40, blond, not skinny, not plump," he quoted from his notes. "Very neat, piano teacher…"

"Music teacher," Bernard corrected. "She doesn't like being called a piano teacher. It's music she teaches."

"Sorry, music teacher… and blind."

"Yes. That's Hannah."

"Do you know how she became blind?" asked Milly. "Was she always blind?"

"No, not always, but I'm not sure how it happened. Something to do with a swimming accident is what I surmised. Seems there was this accident when she was a girl…19 or 20… and she lost her sight. Didn't stop her though."

"You didn't know her then?" asked Romy.

"No. We didn't meet until a couple years later. We went to the same college and met in the student union. She was with a group of friends and I joined them. I didn't even know she was blind until we got up to leave. But I was in love by then. Had to get to know her better." Bernard was quiet for a moment before adding, "That was… 1953, no 1954. We graduated in 1955, her in music, me in coaching."

"Ah, so you're a coach, not a musician. With a school?"

"Yeah, the local high school. Been coaching now for nearly twenty years… well eighteen."

"And you two have a daughter. Is she home?"

"No, she and her friends went swimming. In the seventh grade already. They grow up so fast."

"Doesn't she see her mother?"

"No, Hannah's been sending part of her paycheck to help, but she never visits."

"Mr. Mason," Milly began very slowly, "why did Hannah leave?"

No one moved. The stillness lay thick over the three people trying to untangle a mess that obviously took years to get so snarled up.

Then Bernard spoke. "She told me she felt smothered."

"Smothered?"

"Yes, like her folks used to do when she became blind. They smothered her, were over protective, I guess. One day she just up and told me she needed to breathe. Guess she did the same thing with her parents, just up and left one day, saying they smothered her."

"Didn't you ask where she was going?"

"Couldn't. She left one day while Tanya and I were at school. When I got home, Tanya was crying and looking for her mom. I called everybody I could think of, but she just disappeared — with just a note to tell me not to look for her."

"You didn't think of calling the authorities?"

"Naw. I figured she'd come back in a few days." Bernard sat back and looked into the past. "Or a few weeks, or a few months... now it's six years."

"Would you have any reason to suspect foul play? Do you consider that she might have an enemy?"

"Hannah? God no! She doesn't know how to make enemies. She..."

"Some of her students suggested she was preoccupied in the last few weeks." Milly consulted her notes as she waited for Bernard's response.

"Preoccupied? Maybe she was listening."

"Listening?" Romy looked at Milly with a blank question on his face.

"Listening. Blind people do that. They hear things that we don't hear. And Hannah heard music — a lot — 'music of the Universe', she called it. Nothing I could hear, of course, but it seemed to be in the air, so to speak, just before she left me."

Milly leaned forward. "You say she felt smothered with you before she left. Can you explain that?"

"Nope. Just something she said — *smothered.* I let her do anything she wanted. Gave her plenty of room. Still, there was Tanya's needs. And teenagers can be pretty needy. Even at that, we tried to give her independence, get her to take care of herself so Hannah didn't need to." Bernard shot a glance at Romy that said, *how can you ever know what a woman thinks?*

Milly stood up and extended her hand. "Thank you, Mr. Mason. I think we have a bit more to go on. Oh, can you give me an address or phone number for Hannah's parents?"

"Sorry, they're both gone."

"Any sisters or brothers?" asked Romy, getting to his feet.

"Just Hannah. She was everything to them. Maybe that's why they protected her so much."

"Anyone else we might contact? Friends, old acquaintances?" Milly walked slowly to the front door.

Romy picked up her cue and added, "Old boyfriends?"

Bernard was opening the door for his guests and stopped suddenly showing his anger. His face was close to Romy's as he snarled, "No! No old boyfriends. No friends, period. Hannah was a loner, a sad little blind girl who didn't make friends easily. And while you didn't ask, no, I wasn't her first boyfriend. There had been someone before me, but she never talked about him." Then he swung open the door wide and stood stiffly while his guests passed by.

"Thank you, Mr...." Milly began, but the door had been slammed shut.

Back in Avril, Milly reported to their supervisor and asked, "What now?"

"The college," he told her. "Find out what you can about her job and the students she taught at the college."

DEAD END

Another week passed and the hint of autumn was invading August, just that first wisp of chill that tells the leaves to dry up and turn into glorious colored reminders of summer. By that time, Hannah Mason had been gone nearly seven weeks. Nothing more had turned up at the post office, either in town or at the college.

"We encourage our teachers to use the college postal service," Chancellor Sarah told the detectives. She was walking with them across the campus, breathing deeply the scents of early autumn and late memories.

"That's the building where Hannah taught," she said, pointing to a dark stone building covered with... ivy, what else? No sounds reached their ears from the building.

"Nobody practicing music today?" asked Romy.

"Nobody at school right now," responded Miss Sarah.

"Summer school ended?" Romy asked.

"Yes, last week and the fall term won't begin until mid-September."

"The students all went home before the Fourth of July?" asked Milly.

"Most of them. Some of the summer students stayed over. But most of our student body lives close by and can commute to school."

The trio had arrived at the student union building, where Miss Sarah worked her way up the few steps to the door. Milly offered her arm, but the older woman waved it off. "Exercise is good for me," she puffed. Romy took the steps in two leaps, grabbed the door and pulled it open.

"Over there… the post office," she indicated the grilled window with her hand. Behind the window were rows of letter boxes, mostly empty. In the corner were larger boxes labeled with names of instructors, assistants, and professors. "I don't usually get much mail here; haven't collected mine for several days. Best I pick it up now."

Chancellor Sarah walked over to her box and pulled out a few brochures and envelopes. Her eyes glanced at the return addresses before she gasped and pulled one small envelope from the pack. "Look!" she waved the envelope. "It's from her. It's from Hannah!"

Romy grasped the envelope and held it up to the light. "We can't open it."

"Why not?" asked Milly.

"Yes, why not?" asked Sarah. "It's addressed to me."

"Oh yes. Sorry. I only meant that the law says… you can't… open…" Romy quit talking and handed the envelope back to Sarah.

The old hands worked open the envelope and pulled out the folded paper. It was a simple page of lined note pad paper, written on only one side in big scrawly letters. Sarah read through the message silently before handing the paper to Milly, who read:

Sarah, You probably know by now that I have left the college. Please don't worry about me. I'm all right. Remember that song I was trying to think of? Something was haunting me, the song, something about it that made me want to cry, but I couldn't. I've been wandering about, visiting old haunts, trying to recall what is making me so unhappy, what has been gnawing at my senses. I wish I could tell you that I found it, but I'm not sure. Anyway, I won't be back for fall semester. I'm sorry if this inconveniences the college, or you. Know that I truly regret any trouble I'm causing. Sincerely, Hannah Mason, Music Teacher.

Sarah smiled as Milly returned the letter to her. "She's all right," she said. "Hannah's all right."

"We can't be sure of that," Romy said, sounding skeptical. "Are you sure that is Hannah's handwriting? I thought she was blind? How can she write?"

"Romy, don't…"

"Yes, young man, that is Hannah's handwriting." Sarah drew herself up. "I don't see any reason to doubt her word. She learned to write by holding one finger on the left side of the page and moving it down a bit for each line. This is definitely from her."

"Unless she's been forced to write that note," Milly added.

"But wouldn't there be a ransom note if there was a kidnapping?" Sarah asked quietly. "And there hasn't been one, has there?"

"No, of course not," said Romy. "But that doesn't mean…"

"Miss Sarah, if there has been foul play, Hannah could be in real trouble. We aren't going to close this case until we see and talk to Hannah Mason, until we know the reason for her disappearance. Someone with no reason just ups and leaves a good job, kind friends, a comfortable place to live… it just doesn't make sense." Milly looked closely at the letter in Sarah's hand. "Can we take this with us?"

"Why, of course."

"The postmark…" Romy grabbed at the envelope.

"Already thought of it, Sherlock," said Milly. "It's postmarked Avril, two weeks ago."

"Another dead-end."

"At least we have reason to believe she's alive," said Milly. "Let's go."

"Thank you, Miss Sarah," said Romy, bowing slightly to the woman. "You'll be hearing from us as soon as we can offer more information."

The two FBI agents returned to their car and drove back to their hotel headquarters. Not the kind of HQ seen in movies, the room was part of the three-room suite they reserved for their stay. In a small town like Avril, a "three room suite" just meant three rooms with connecting doors. They sat at the table near the window.

"Room service?" suggested Milly.

"Yeah, something cool… and filling."

"Can't wait for dinner?"

"Didn't have lunch."

Milly went to the phone and ordered sandwiches, cole slaw and iced tea.

"Beer," called Romy. "Bottle of brew for me."

"And one beer," Milly added, putting down the phone. "Okay, where are we — and what do we tell the boss?"

Both the detectives pulled out their notepads and flipped through the pages.

"No reason, no background, no clues to where she is. Nothing! What the hell is going on? We're just where we were weeks ago." Romy slapped down his notepad and began to pace.

"We have clues. Bernard gave us something."

"Wouldn't you think he'd have heard from her — something?"

"Yet, she's been gone six years. And he still seems to care about her."

"You think so? I didn't think he even noticed she was gone."

"Wish we'd had a chance to talk to the kid."

"Do you think she could add anything to this dead-end case?"

"Maybe. Maybe we ought to go back."

"Maybe we ought to…" a knock at the door interrupted their argument. "There's my beer. I'll get it!"

When two people work together, a special relationship develops which can be either hostile and defiant, or friendly and helpful, or intimate and difficult. Milly and Romy had been working as partners for more than five years and had grown into the friendly and helpful arena, while retaining a bit of hostility and confrontation. They teased each other and enjoyed getting a one-up on the partner. Still, their work brought results. Over the years they had found a number of missing people — some living and some otherwise.

Romy sometimes played the blundering foil to Milly's incisive observation. Other times, he wasn't so sure that he was "playing." Milly seemed so capable that Romy often doubted his wisdom. The one thing he could do better than anyone else on the force was add up the clues and come up with answers. Not this time.

Romy would be 35 on his next birthday and wondered if he'd ever find a mate. On his off time, he returned to his home in Chicago, looked up old friends and all but begged to be "fixed up" with a date. Still, nothing gelled. And now his old friends were beginning to divorce each other, and he didn't feel comfortable picking up his friends' discarded wives.

As an agent of the FBI, Romy had to travel a lot and remain on duty or on call most of the time. And while he hankered after a long-term relationship — a wife (okay, he actually used the word once) — he hadn't found the woman who could put up with his weird schedule.

As for Milly, she was nearing retirement. She'd turn 55 on her next birthday. She didn't miss the home life her sister enjoyed with a husband and five children; she did give it a thought once in a while. Maybe she should have had one child, or two. Like Romy, and most agents, she just didn't have the time to look up a spouse.

Milly's family was from the South and had expected her to be married and "settled down" by the age of 20. Imagine their surprise, indignation, opposition, and desperation when she was accepted into the FBI Academy. She loves the work, loves solving puzzles and working out clues.

Romy was intrigued with the fact she could complete the *New York Times* Sunday Crossword in less than an hour.

Both of these agents loved good food, but their ideas of "good food" varied. Milly preferred fish and chicken, with iced tea; Romy went for pizza and tacos and beer. And yet there were times they split the difference and enjoyed French cuisine at a trendy place in DC.

There was never any intimacy between them that went any closer than the intimacy of brother and sister. The best part was their ability to work as a team. In DC, they were considered the best in the business — quiet, efficient, clever — and they got results.

The case of Hannah Mason, however, had them stumped. Not only could they discern no patterns, there seemed to be no reason for her disappearance, and only a single husband and child to be concerned (and even they didn't seem to care much).

SOL U TION

"Why do we care about this woman? Why are we even doing this investigation?"

"Because we were called in by the local authorities. Something's been bothering me. Remember that young woman who was her student, the neighbor girl, Cal… cutta, or something… Calpurnia. Her name's Calpurnia."

"Not a name for a girl. Wonder where she got it. You were saying?"

"Not important." Milly was flipping pages of her notebook, back to the day they arrived. "Cal said they had talked about the past on the porch that day — the Fourth. They talked about family and neighbors and being close to someone. They talked about the opera. And…" she read a few more lines, "…and Cal talked about running away…" Milly looked up. "Do you think?"

"I think! First thing tomorrow, let's go back to Hannah's house and take another look. Maybe we can find something that'll give us a clue… something we've missed."

The door was still unlocked as the FBI duo entered Hannah's house the next morning. Everything in the house remained as it was, with slightly more dust than before. The agents spent a long time going over everything, even bringing in lunch to eat while they pondered.

They settled in the kitchen with a pizza. Milly heated water for tea while Romy hunted for a pizza slicer. As Millie waited for the water to boil, she casually turned to the radio sitting on the counter. "Music okay?" she asked.

"Sure," Romy muttered, not really caring very much.

Millie turned the switch, but nothing happened. No sound. She checked to be sure the radio was plugged in; it was. She was about to turn it off when a song began to play. "Strange music for this time of day," she said.

Looking closer, she almost squealed when she noticed that the "radio" wasn't a radio. "It's a player!" she called to Romy. "Listen! It's playing a song I think I know… let me see… what the heck is the name of that tune?"

"Sounds mushy to me, the kind silly romantic girls play. Remember that coed at that college in Ohio when we were looking for…"

"Shhhh!" hissed Milly. "Shush and listen."

The two leaned over the player, Milly humming the familiar tune, until she came to the last line. Her memory kicked in and she sang aloud, "…*to renew old memories.* Sentimental Journey! That's the song."

As the words flooded back, she started over. "*Gonna take a sentimental journey…* Get it? That's what Calpurnia was talking about. She has gone back… somewhere she once lived… to recall better times, to 'renew memories'."

"You could be right. That fits with what Mr. Mason said, about some earlier love he didn't know."

"Everything is clicking into place. She was lonely, melancholy perhaps, and ever the romantic musician. She simply went looking to recapture an earlier moment of happiness. Case closed!"

The two agents pulled out notebooks, reviewed their jottings, and feverishly wrote out a report while finishing the pizza. The report carefully laid out their conclusion that the music teacher longed for something lost long ago and had headed back... to... where? (Wherever it happened.)

They carefully cleaned up the crumbs and wiped off the table, leaving the house as neat as they found it.

Back at the office, they called the supervisor and advanced their conclusion, adding that their report would be in the mail that afternoon.

Harriet Mason fingered the certificate she kept hidden in her purse. She sat on a bench in the sun in the park, seemingly waiting for the autumn leaves to finish falling. She hadn't been sitting long when a man shuffled through the dry leaves and sat down beside her. Neither spoke; they didn't have to; they could feel each others presence.

"She's well," Harriet said. "My husband takes very good care of her. I think she's going to be a musician too."

"Don't see why not," the man offered. "Seeing as how both her parents are musicians."

They reached out their hands then, sliding them along the sun-warmed bench, and held each other as they listened to the music that encircled them.

LIFE IS A BIRD

4 a.m.   Get up early and sing. Find something to eat. Sing some more.

Call to a friend; answer the friend.

6 a.m.   Preen the feathers; chirp a bit; fly and dive and swoop and call.

7 a.m.   Find more to eat. Wash it down with a drink from a pool.

8 a.m.   Fly about with friends; flit about in a bird bath.

Twitter and tweet for yourself.

10 a.m. Pick a fight; fly off and make up. Sing.

Fend off a larger bird; squawk at a squirrel.

Noon: Pull up a worm; catch a bug on the fly.

3 p.m.   Sip from a mud puddle.

7 p.m.   Find a late snack, sing a lullaby, sleep.

"How like the bird's life is mine," croaked Sylvia as she addressed that strange old woman in the mirror. "Routine! That's what it is. Just move the clock ahead a few hours – like they do every spring — and there I am. Change the time line of the birds and the rest is me."

The old woman doesn't address her words to anyone in particular. They're mostly thoughts that flit through her head. "Don't believe me, huh?" Sylvia's days can be routine. "Take a look at what I did yesterday."

4 a.m. Make a trip to the bathroom and go back to bed. Lie still and try to return to that great dream; ponder the things-to-do list; remember what life was like when… forget that… you'll just make yourself cry again. Listen to

the birds; they're awake now. Hum a bit of that tune you and he used to dance to. Wonder if he's still alive... somewhere.

6 a.m. At last, a good dream. Wonder what it was about. Wish I could remember them. Might as well pull myself out of bed. Get dressed; the orange sweatsuit is clean. Comb my hair — Jonathan might come by today. Wouldn't want my son to think I'm letting myself go. I do hope he's settling down to fatherhood; god knows it took him long enough. He seems happy, but... wonder if I remembered to pick up fresh eggs yesterday.

8 a.m. Not as forgetful as Amelia says I am. The eggs were exactly right. Will that girl ever get a real job and put her painting aside? Must remember to call her and... must remember to buy butter. I'm sure the birds don't worry about such things; they just hone in on a bug and there's breakfast. And they don't have to worry about which fat worm is going to ruin their figure.

10 a.m. Amelia called to shout at me for half an hour about why I haven't called her lately. My darling daughter tells me one minute not to bother her when she's painting, and the next she yowls about not calling. Jonathan called to ask about the baby's rash. Why doesn't he ask his wife? Hauled out the piano and played for a bit. Found one I could sing, even if the voice is gone. Where does a voice go when you get old? And why?

Noon: Amelia showed up with takeout lunch, tacos. I tried to sing my song to her, but she shushed me. The kids always shush me when I'm trying to sing. Do I sound that bad? Anyway, the lunch was nice and we hugged and parted friends. She asked about how I got along with *my* mother and I had forgotten how bad things got before I left home. Do daughters and mothers ever get over the growing up process? "Mom, I'm a grown woman; leave me alone."

3 p.m. Took my walk. Gotta walk, Jonathan keeps nagging. I've found the perfect trail. It leads to the coffee shop about five blocks away. I can rest there a bit and enjoy a quiet cuppa before returning home. Why doesn't Jonathan ever evoke memories of my father? Raising boys obviously is different. Annabelle called and wants to take me to lunch tomorrow. I'll go, but reluctantly. She complains too much about her aches and pains, and sometimes I feel she hates me for staying healthy. It's the walking, I guess.

7 p.m. The birds have quieted down. Dozed off, I imagine. Almost time for Jeopardy! (you have to put that exclamation mark in there). Got so hungry after my walk, I snacked. Still hungry at dinnertime, and worms didn't appeal to me. Put together a plate of mac and cheese with a lovely salad, followed by a new frozen dairy dessert, caramel-vanilla. I wonder if birds ever crave ice cream.

11 p.m. Sleepy time at last, although I know I'll get to bed and lie awake for a time. I'll sing that song again, the one he and I used to sing all those years ago. Wonder whatever happened to him. I know! I'll hum a lullaby; that oughta close my eyes. And I'll add that line about waking up again. After all, I have to keep up with the birds. Hmmmm. Goodnight, world!

Sylvia lived on for several more months. I believe she died the fall weekend we moved the clocks back. She had made peace with her children, loved the new grandchild to bits, and learned to appreciate her daughter's artistic talent. She stopped walking a couple months ago. Too hard on her knees, she said. Then one night she went to bed and must have been enjoying a dream too much to wake up. Besides, the birds had stopped singing and the weather had turned cold.

AUNT 29, NIECE 6
JUST TALKING

Aunt, at 29: Can you tell me what's in the glass?

    Niece at 6: Water.

Do you know what water is?

    Wet.

And what else?

    Clear and it's cold and hot.

Do you know where water comes from?

    From the sea?

How is it different?

    'Cause it comes from the rain?

The water in the cup, where did I get that from?

    The rain? No, from the sink.

From the sink. Where does water come in from the sink?

    From rain? In the drain. In the sidewalk, and then it goes through the waterworks.

What's the waterworks?

    Well you see, they go with the water through the drain, through the sink then into a cup.

What is snow made of?

    Raindrops.

Where does it come from?

    The sky.

Where does the rain comes from? How does it get there?

God, rain clouds.

God and rain clouds?

I mean rain clouds.

Do you know what rain clouds are made of?

Fluffy.

What about ice?

Ice is made out of water.

And how is it different from water in the cup?

'Cause it's froze.

How did it get frozen?

Refrigerator.

Is it like the ice that you find outside when it's wintertime?

Yes.

Is it like ice at the ice skating rink?

Yes.

Do you know how ice is made?

You put water in the pond and then the snow makes it freeze up. And you put snow in the water and then it turns into ice. Or in the refrigerator, in the freezer. You put water into the freezer and then you take it out and when you want to use it, it turns into ice.

Can you swim in water?

Yes.

How do you come to swim in water?

'Cause you get vacation in spring and summer.

Is that the only time you can swim in water?

Yes.

Do you absorb water when you swim? Do you come out looking bigger?

No.

What happens when you sweat?

Water is sweat.

Is that water leaving your body?

But it comes back.

What about spit?

I don't know.

What is spit?

Germ water.

Why is it germ water?

'Cause you have germs in your stomach.

When you take a shower, or a bath, when you can't see 'cause there's stuff in the air? Where does that come from?

It's steam! When you take warm water or hot water in the shower, it makes the steam go all around.

How do you think all that steam gets out of the water?

When you turn it on and the water goes (motions hand in waves)…

So the steam goes up?

Yeah.

Why?

Because. I don't know why.

Is there anything else you know about water?

No.

What happens when you water the lawn?

It goes in the soil.

And then where?

The roots… of the plants.

Do you know anything about the river?

I know something about the river. It has lots of fish.

Do you think fish like the water?

Yeah.

Could fish live on land?

Yeah. In a fishbowl.

How much do you love your Auntie?

A whole lot.

Is that all? And how beautiful is she?

Very beautiful.

And how smart is she?

Very smart.

And what else?

And she wears sweatpants sometimes. And she loves me a lot. One million billion,

I think it's more than that.

One trillion?

Hugs and kisses and thank you for your help.

COUNTER ENCOUNTER

(Breveloquence Essay

A challenge to write a story in 100 words)

The morning sun sparkled in her eyes. "Cream?" she asked.

"Thanks, no," he answered.

"Toast? Sweet roll?"

"Just coffee." He wanted only to feast on her sweet eyes, deep ponds of blue-gray, joyous eyes hinting at life's promises.

Many years later... many, many years... he returned to those glorious eyes, now framed with gray, still sparkling with mystery.

"Coffee?" She whisked up the bones of steak and peel of baked potato. The orange sun, slipping behind the hills, shone from the depth of her merry blue-gray eyes.

"Yes, thanks."

"Cream?" Then, "You've been here before?"

"Oh yes," he said. "All my life."

HALLOWEEN

Town kids all know the best Halloween treats are from the big house on the hill at the edge of town. That's where Sunday Weeks lives with her cats, her orchard, and a couple of horses. They call her Miss Rich Witch, sometimes Miss Rich Bitch behind her back, but they always get special treats, like warm cookies straight from her oven and cold apples just picked from her orchard. Sometimes she has a couple of horses saddled for them to ride.

Generous? Kind? We all thought so. Sunday Weeks had become the town legend. They named the library after her, and the school, and even reconsidered renaming the town when she donated a huge amount of money to repaint the courthouse.

But Sunday wasn't always that rich. She grew up on the old Weeks farm out in the valley. It wasn't much of a farm at first, but the Weeks always had been good at growing things — corn, hops, horses and kids. They had seven of those kids, in all, each named for a day of the week.

Monday was the oldest; he grew into a strapping man who took over running the farm when Pa got too old. Then came Tuesday, a pretty woman who became her mother's protégé in the kitchen. Wednesday was a dickens of a kid and grew up to become an artist who sold a few paintings of the farm. Thursday was the family brain. Friday was the weird one, always trying to blow things up with his concoctions. And Saturday. Ah Saturday, the dancer who would have danced her way into the big time if she hadn't developed stage fright. Couldn't stand to have folks watch her dance, so she pirouetted and kicked her way around the barn and the cornfield.

Sunday was the last born. Ma and Pa Weeks rested after she came into the world. Sunday was the one who received the benefit of all the other kids — got to wear their clothes, play with their toys, take over their chores as they moved out of the house. She was also the quiet one. Nobody ever knew what was going on inside her little red head.

Growing up was probably the easiest part for Sunday. She got fed every day, almost, and had things to do to keep her busy. She never went to college, because the family had run out of money by the time she was old enough. Her happiest time was at Halloween, after the fall harvest, when all the family got together to celebrate their favorite holiday. Every year, until about seven or eight years ago.

That's when the Weeks began to ail. Ma and Pa. Ma took sick first, probably worn out from raising seven kids and keeping them fed and their clothes clean. Ma used to can most of their food in the fall, make clothes during the winter, plant her garden each spring, and spend summers weeding and tending and nurturing. She just ran out of steam and took to her bed. She died just after Christmas. Pa was so distraught, and tired too, I reckon, that he died just after spring planting the following year.

By then the farm was doing very well, especially the hops crops. When Pa's will was read, the kids realized the farm was worth a nice bundle of money. Naturally, Pa left the farm to all of them, to be divided equally. He also made sure that the farm share of each kid would be divided among the others upon their deaths.

Monday continued to run the farm, and each fall he divided the hops profits with his brothers and sisters. The year after Ma and Pa died, he and Sunday were the only two living on the farm. Tuesday had married, moved out, and started her own family. Wednesday moved to the city and sold her artistic talents to an ad agency. Thursday went on to college and became a doctor, a plastic surgeon, I think, in a bigger city. Friday took over the town pharmacy. And

Saturday continued to dance in the cornfield. Eventually, she attracted a hobo passing through town and they ran off to see the world.

They all came back, however, to spend Halloween in the family home. Sunday, with the help of Tuesday, would cook gigantic meals and they'd all sit around the huge table and remember Ma and Pa and their growing up days — the good and the bad.

Then we townies started to notice a coincidence of events.

Dr. Thursday was the first to pass into another world — a few days after Halloween, oh about six years ago, from what appeared to be a mild upset stomach. (Everyone knows that doctors don't get proper health treatment.)

The following year Saturday, just back from a trek to Asia, complained of strange numbness in her legs. She died a week later — presumably from some bug she picked up in her travels.

Then, four years ago Wednesday came down with a malady just before the big pre-Christmas ad campaign, and just after Halloween. She complained of headaches and altered sight just before she died.

Friday, the pharmacist, had always tried to cure his own ailments. When he came down with a variety of symptoms, they didn't respond to any of his remedies, and he died the next year.

Monday and Tuesday joined Sunday for a very quiet Halloween two years ago. After dinner, Tuesday told her family she wasn't feeling well and went to an upstairs bedroom to rest. She never came down. Last year, yes, just a year ago, Monday sold the farm — for a big pile of cash and an ongoing share in the hops crops. He and Sunday bought that big house on the hill and moved in, bringing only a couple of their best horses. They cleared out the orchard and were enjoying their first Halloween in the house when Monday caught some kind of flu and ran out of breath.

Sunday, the quiet one, had received her last gift from the other kids — an annual income from the hops and a huge house furnished with things she bought brand new. There were computers and TVs and other electronic toys, a closet full of new clothes, and a freezer full of her favorite food — it was all hers.

Everybody in town knows what a tragic figure lives in that big old house on the hill on the edge of town, and they still enjoy her generosity. But they have never figured out what is going on inside her little red head.

JIM

You know the bar I go to after work when I have some spare time — that one that was remodeled out of an old fire station? Engine No. 9, it's called now, with fancy paneled walls, ceiling fans, a long well-stocked bar and a few tables around the TV set. It's my place, the place I go to relax after a hard day working for the boss, the place that offers a sort of quiet, a cold pint, and occasionally someone interesting to talk with.

Usually, I meet my friend Rick there. Since I get off at three most afternoons and he doesn't go to work until eight in the evening, we have time to let off steam, talk about music, and down a beer or two. Rick and I met years ago when we both worked for a record store. He's a Beatles fan and I'm a Rush connoisseur. We argue a lot about which group made better music, but we always come to a draw. There's no accounting for taste.

That day we met as usual, about 3:15. I had already ordered when Rick settled down on the stool next to me.

"I see our friend is here again," he said, pointing to the strange little man sitting at a nearby table. He had papers strewn out in front of him and appeared to be a teacher marking lessons as he sipped on a brew.

"Don't you have to wonder why he's here?"

"Yeah. If he's a teacher or something, he should be doing this at home."

We both smiled then and said, almost together, "And get that toup!"

The man wore a very bad wig that covered the entire top of his head and drooped a bit onto his forehead. His squinty eyes peered out from under the thatch. He was at least 60, probably nearing retirement. But the most noticeable part of him were his boots, a pair of ankle-high polished gentleman's boots, long out of style. We had noticed him before, at the same table with papers and pen.

"Teacher! Yup! He's got to be a teacher. But why here?"

"He's afraid to go home?"

"Maybe. I'd bet he's got no home."

"Yeah? Next beer's on me if it's not his fear." I was getting brave after my second glass.

"You're on, Stevo," Rick replied as he shook my hand. "But how'll we know?"

We didn't have to wait. Almost as if he had heard us, the man stood and approached the bar. Trying to look nonchalant, he ordered another beer, then turned to us. "Hello," he said, his squinty eyes lowered and his mouth trying to form a smile. "My name's Jim. I see you gentlemen here often. You brothers or something?"

"Brothers? Oh no…" Rick began.

"Well, sorta," I added. "We're good friends. Have been for years. I'm Steve; this is Rick. Hi Jim. Good to meetcha."

"Want to join us?" Rick asked. My head snapped towards him and my eyes asked *why*, but Rick went on. "Bring your papers over and join us."

"Might be easier if you guys sat at my table," Jim offered.

We grabbed our glasses and moved to his table as Jim packed up his papers and returned them to a scruffy looking briefcase.

We asked a few leading questions and quickly learned that yes, he was a teacher, at the nearby private high school. He taught music, band, chorus, and gave private piano lessons. He seemed very proud of his longstanding career at the same school. Nearly 30 years. It was my experience that gave rise to the question of his retirement. I knew that many teachers were given "early retirement" or laid off before their pensions kicked in, but I didn't say anything.

It wasn't long before our talk included friendly discussions about the merits of the Beatles and my Rush guys. Of course, Jim favored the March King, Sousa. He seemed impressed that Rick still had plastic recordings of Beatle music, and more impressed when he learned how he had recently sold an old recording online for four times what he'd paid for it.

"Gee, $150 bucks! Somebody actually paid that much for an old record?"

"Not just an old record," Rick said, rising to his full height. He would not be insulted by a stranger.

"I didn't mean anything," Jim quickly countered. "It just seems like good fortune, actually.

We didn't even discuss Rush. The old guy had never heard of them. We moved our talk to the bar service, the pretty barmaid, and the latest football game, although the latter subject didn't seem to interest any of us. We drank our beer.

"You married? Either of you?" Jim asked after a moment's silence.

"I am. My wife is a city accountant," Rick said.

"And what do you do?"

"Oh, this and that. Mostly I work with a local band and other pick-up bands. And I work part-time in a record store."

"Not much business, is there? I mean, who buys records in a store anymore?" Jim turned abruptly to me and asked, "And what do you do, Steve?"

I pointed to my shirt logo. "I own my own landscape business."

"Oh, you like the outdoors. No wonder you have such a nice tan."

"Didn't think of it that way, but I guess so. Yeah, I like working outdoors."

"Married?" he asked, a sound of hope in his voice.

"Not any more. Divorced. Free as a bird."

"God, you sound almost happy about it. I'm divorced too… well not just yet… waiting for the final papers. My wife left almost a year ago. Just up and walked out after thirty years of marriage."

"No reason?" Rick asked.

"None. Just up and left. Went back East to stay with her family. Then she sent the papers."

"You don't seem too happy about that," I commented idly. But he bristled at the words.

"Happy? Happy? I should be happy? My dear wife just up and left. No! I am not happy, not in the least. I am…" but he couldn't come up with the right words. I guessed that he didn't know how to identify his emotions. I waved at Sally to ask for our bill.

A long silence followed, broken only when Sally handed us our tabs. "See you guys tomorrow," she called cheerily.

Rick and I paid up and walked away, leaving Jim fumbling to retrieve his papers from his briefcase. Outside, I turned to Rick and held out my hand. "Did we have an actual bet on this? Didn't I tell you he was afraid to go home? Nobody there. Empty silence. Lonely rooms. You owe me a beer, Rick."

"Tomorrow, Stevo!" Rick waved me off and headed for his car. "See ya tomorrow."

For the next few days, Jim joined Rick and me at the Engine House for our afternoon beer, regaling us with stories of his youth. He described his adventures as he sailed around the world, was almost shanghaied in Jamaica, lost his ship in the North Sea, received a medal of honor for service in Nam, hung out with a couple of '80s Russians who later turned out to be spies — that kind of stuff.

We listened, but we didn't believe half of what he continued to tell us. It wasn't long before we were doubting everything he said. Nobody had a life that interesting and ended up with a thirty-year teaching career at a small high school in the Northwest. But we let him talk.

In between Jim's escapades, Rick and I talked about our music preferences, teasing one another a bit about what we liked and didn't like. We were old friends, and old friends, good friends, tease each other about silly stuff.

Soon Jim offered his own kind of teasing. Except his words had an edge to them, a kind of taunting, deprecating edge that wasn't the fun teasing, but the sarcastic poking. It's hard to put your finger on it. But we certainly felt the anger that was coming through.

"Did he get to you with that dig about your Canadian strummers?" Rick asked one day as we left the bar.

"Not really… well, yes, he did. I wasn't sure if I heard exactly what he meant, but if you noticed, then I was right. He wasn't being playful; he was making a snide remark."

"I wasn't sure either. He has such a way with his words, it's hard to know if he's kidding or criticizing."

We mentioned it; we forgot about it. Probably just a misunderstanding of words. Probably just a bad day at school, or more bad news from his missus.

Still, the jibes increased. And my irritation increased, since the jibes most often were aimed at me. He downplayed my work, my interest in music, my talk of writing a blog online, my girlfriends that came and went. But most of all, he challenged my information.

In a weird discussion about pianos one day, I mentioned that Steinways were all made by hand, and Jim bristled. "You are definitely wrong, sir," he said. "They may be put together by hand, but they are manufactured. The parts are manufactured, Steve."

"I don't think so, Jim. Seems I read this article in *Time* magazine about how they're made by hand, parts and all. The article said it takes a year to make a single piano."

"Well that just doesn't make sense," Jim replied. "How can they sell pianos all over the world if it takes a year to make one piano? By hand or not?"

"I presume they work on more than one at a time, but each one takes a year to complete. I'm sure of that."

Suddenly Jim jumped up from our table, stuffed a bunch of papers in his briefcase and stomped out of Engine No. 9.

The next day, Rick had called to say he was tied up and couldn't join me. I had endured a hard day planting trees in the rain, and I welcomed the quiet of the bar and the comfort of a beer alone. I had forgotten about Jim. But there he was, sitting at his table.

"Guess you've called your pal, huh?" he growled as I walked by.

"What do you mean?" I asked.

"Your pal, Rick. Guess you've called him already, huh?"

I wasn't sure what he was asking, and continued to walk up to the bar, where I grabbed a stool and reached over for the crossword puzzle. Nobody ever worked on it – so it was free for me to occupy my head as I sipped my beer. Sally knew not to bother me on such days. After all, this was "my bar" and I felt like I could be comfortable here.

I had filled in only about three words when Jim walked over. "Your buddy not coming? Did I scare him off?"

"What do you mean, Jim?" I was trying to be polite. After all, he was a few years older than me, well, almost old enough to be my father. And I always tried to be polite with my father.

"You working the crossword puzzle?" He changed the subject.

"Well, yes."

"You good at crossword puzzles?" The poor man was trying to open a conversation, but I wasn't falling for it.

"Yup!" was all I would say.

Jim slid onto the stool next to mine and began his story all over again, about how his wife had left for no reason, how he couldn't coax her back, and how great he was at his job. He went into another tirade about all the experience he had as a musician "in the good old days" and how he had worked hard to earn a living at what he was good at.

Now I'm not a psychiatrist. Maybe a kind of philosopher, but not a psycho person. It wasn't difficult to understand that Jim had some problems. He didn't like to be upstaged; he didn't like to be wrong; he didn't like to be criticized; and he didn't like to be teased. That much was clear. And, he didn't like to be ignored.

He finished his beer, packed up his papers, and walked out of the bar. I returned to my crosswords.

When I next saw Rick, a day or two later, I told him about this strange discussion. You know Jim, always stretching to be friendly, always trying to be smart, always trying to interject something witty, and failing. I suggested to Rick that he reminded me a bit of my father.

"I knew your father. Remember when he visited you a few years ago? If you want my opinion, you may have a problem here too. Are you taking out your issues with your dad on Jim?"

"You weren't here, Rick. You didn't hear the way he talked to me. When you're here, when it's the three of us, he's a completely different fellow. He's congenial, polite, and controlled. The other day he definitely had lost it. He was mean. He was rude. He was close to yelling at me."

"I've never heard him raise his voice. Are you sure?"

"Oh jeez, you're questioning me? You know, I wouldn't be a bit surprised if Jim didn't pick up a machine gun one of these days and shoot a bunch of people — maybe the people in this bar. You think? You don't believe what I'm telling you. Well, then believe this. I'm not taking any more of his insinuations, his little remarks, his mean jabs at me. I think he likes you better than he likes… no, that isn't what I mean."

"Or maybe it is. Maybe you're jealous of him. Maybe you think I favor him over you. Come on, man, you know better than that. We've been friends for too long."

"Maybe that's it — too long. Maybe I ought to just leave the two of you alone." I picked up my gear, threw some money on the bar, and walked away.

That was more than a month ago. I haven't answered any of Rick's calls, nor returned a couple of emails that apologized. I stewed by myself, picking up a six-pack and returning to my apartment after work, alone.

Was I fighting my father — three years after he died? Was I mistaking Jim for my father when I suggested he liked my friend better than me? Was I jealous? Jeez, have I lost it?

I had to answer that other question. Was this a power play between Jim and me, or did I just not like the guy? He dressed funny. He looked funny. He talked formally. He lied openly. He was always right. And he just plain annoyed the hell out of me.

Why, you may ask, didn't we just up and find another bar to hang out after work? My answer is that I like this place. Engine No. 9 is my kind of place, friendly, comfortable, noninvasive, and I can work out the crosswords here in peace. If only Jim hadn't come along.

I'm a strong believer in the power of Zen, and recognize the need to keep the energy around me positive. Jim upset that energy by contributing a whole pile of negative shit.

The next afternoon, I had a plan to establish my space and my rules. I strode into Engine No. 9 about 3:15, sat at the bar, ordered a beer, and started the crossword. Within minutes, Jim walked in. I didn't turn my head, just continued to fill in letters on the puzzle.

"Hello, my good man," he said cheerily. "Haven't seen you in these parts for a while. Have you been sick?"

"Hi," I answered, without looking up.

"Where's your buddy Rick? Is he coming?"

I shrugged my shoulders, and continued to write.

"Doing your crossword?"

I didn't answer.

"Got my divorce papers yesterday. You know the feeling?"

I said nothing.

"I think I'll retire at the end of the year. I'm hearing rumors of lay-offs and early retirement. I can do that. Travel maybe." He seemed to be talking to himself, setting up some plans for the rest of his life. I didn't interfere.

He rambled on for a few minutes as I gulped down the last of my beer, motioned to Sally for my bill, paid it, and got up to leave.

"So, you're leaving?"

What could I answer? Didn't it seem clear?

Yes, I'm leaving — I'm leaving you to straighten out your own life and let me live mine. I'm leaving you behind to bother somebody else. I'm leaving behind me the memories of my father and of my own marriage, and of all the shitty stuff you've been handing me.

I'm outta here!

THE NIGHT BEFORE CHRISTMAS

THE PhD VERSION

APOLOGIES TO CLEMENT CLARKE MOORE

(BY ANONYMOUS)

'Twas the nocturnal segment of the diurnal period preceding the annual Yuletide celebration, and throughout our place of residence, kinetic activity was not in evidence among the possessors of this potential, including that species of domestic rodent known as Mus musculus.

Hosiery was meticulously suspended from the forward edge of the wood-burning caloric apparatus, pursuant to our anticipatory pleasure regarding an imminent visitation from an eccentric philanthropist among whose folkloric appellations is the honorific title of St. Nicholas.

The prepubescent siblings, comfortably ensconced in their respective accommodations of repose, were experiencing subconscious visual hallucinations of variegated fruit confections moving rhythmically through their cerebra.

My conjugal partner and I, attired in our nocturnal cranial coverings, were about to take slumberous advantage of the hibernal darkness when upon the arenaceous exterior portion of the grounds there ascended such a cacophony of dissonance that I felt compelled to arise with alacrity from my place of repose for the purpose of ascertaining the precise source thereof.

Hastening to the casement, I forthwith opened the barriers sealing the fenestration, noting thereupon that the lunar brilliance without, reflected as it was on the surface of a recent crystalline aqueous precipitation, might be said to rival that of the solar meridian itself — thus permitting my incredulous optical sensor to peruse a miniature airborne runnered conveyance drawn by an octet of diminutive specimens of the genus Rangifer, piloted by a minuscule, aged chauffeur so ebullient and nimble that it became instantly apparent to me that he was indeed our anticipated caller.

With his undulate motive power traveling at what may possibly have been more vertiginous velocity than patriotic alar predators, he vociferated loudly, expelled breath musically through contracted labia, and addressed each of the octet by his or her respective cognomen… "Now Dasher, now Dancer…" et al… guiding them to the uppermost exterior level of our abode, through which structure I could readily distinguish the concatenations of each of the 32 cloven pedal extremities.

As I retracted my cranium from its erstwhile location, and was performing a 180-degree pivot, our distinguished visitant achieved — with utmost celerity and via a downward leap — entry by way of the smoke passage. He was clad entirely in animal pelts soiled by the ebon residue from the oxidations of carboniferous fuels which had accumulated on the walls thereof.

His resemblance to a street vendor I attributed largely to the plethora of assorted playthings, which he bore dorsally in a commodious cloth receptacle. His orbs were scintillant with reflected luminosity, while his submaxillary dermal indentations gave every evidence of engaging amiability.

The capillaries of his molar regions and nasal aptenance were engorged with blood which suffused the subcutaneous layers, the former approximating the coloration of Albion's floral emblem, the latter that of the Prunus avium, or sweet cherry.

His amusing sub- and supra labials resembled nothing so much as a common loop knot, and their ambient hirsute facial adornment appeared like small, tabular and columnar crystals of frozen water. Clenched firmly between his incisors was a smoking-piece whose gray fumes, forming a tenuous ellipse about his occiput, were suggestive of a decorative seasonal circlet of holly. His visage was wider than it was high, and when he waxed audibly mirthful, his corpulent abdominal region undulated in the manner of impectinated fruit syrup in a hemispherical container.

Without utterance and with dispatch, he commenced filling the aforementioned hosiery with articles of merchandise extracted from his aforementioned previously dorsally transported cloth receptacle.

Upon completion of this task, he executed an abrupt about-face, placed a single manual digit in lateral juxtaposition to his olfactory organ, inclined his cranium forward in a gesture of leave-taking, and forthwith affected his egress by renegotiating (in reverse) the smoke passage.

He then propelled himself in a short vector onto his conveyance, directed a musical expulsion of air through his contracted oral sphincter to the antlered quadrupeds of burden, and proceeded to soar aloft in a movement hitherto observable chiefly among the seed-bearing portions of a common weed.

But I overheard his parting exclamation, audible immediately prior to his vesiculation beyond the limits of visibility:

"Ecstatic Yuletides to the planetary constituency, and to that self-same assemblage my sincerest wishes for a salubriously beneficial and gratifyingly pleasurable period between sunset and dawn."

[This is another of those free-floating parodies that fill the Internet. Ask for parodies and you'll find all kinds of them. This is my favorite.]

New Years Eve 2000

If you were alive in 1999, you remember the turmoil surrounding the approach of New Years Eve and the introduction of a new millennium. Actually, the new millennium wasn't scheduled until 2001, but who cared. The calendars were being flipped into the 2000s.

Fears flew rampantly about the possibilities: computers would fail; airplanes would fall down; businesses would fall apart; and most seriously, the world and its human contents would disintegrate. Oh the pain and misery that lay in store.

And what did those human contents do? They rushed to reserve rooms at the Waldorf-Astoria in New York, schedule parties at Seattle's Space Needle, and plan exotic trips they hadn't had time for during the twentieth century.

Writers, like me, had a heyday as magazines and newspapers (and that new commodity called the Internet) eagerly sought "millennia stories". Here are a few ideas for stories of *struggle, calamity, wonder,* and *magic* that popped into my head. (Notes like these often end up in drop-dead movies.)

Here's To You! — The Waldorf-Astoria (Struggle)

Reservations clerks begin receiving calls on New Years Day 1995, reserving rooms for New Years 2000. The hotel fills up quickly, and a waiting list is begun. The clerks console callers with hope that in the five years until 2000 a few people will change their minds, some will move away or go broke, some will become ill, and some may even die, thus shortening the list.

A computer hacker learns he is placed 23rd on the list. Desperate for a reservation (I mean *desperate*!), he hacks into the hotel's computer system and learns the identity of the 22 reservations ahead of him. Slowly — he has five years — he shortens the waiting list by doing away with (offing, snuffing out, killing) those ahead of him. By Christmas 1999, the hacker has moved up on the waiting list, with only one, a woman named Mary Holly, in his way. Fine! He'll knock her off at the last minute when she appears.

Getting High — The Space Needle (Calamity)

A large corporation decides to throw a New Millennium party at the Space Needle and books the whole thing for New Years Eve 2000. They're criticized for monopolizing the space, but keep the reservations. They want bragging rights to entering the century "on top" and staying there.

On the big night, just before midnight, someone notices the lights in Tacoma jiggling, then those in Fife, and Des Moines, and Kent — and Everett and Lynnwood and Bothel — and Bellevue and Redmond and... all around them lights in the greater Seattle area are shifting back and forth then disappearing into blackness.

Oh the irony, guess who is experiencing an earthquake — a big one — and just when the party is getting started?

Toast to the Past — Cruise to Egypt (Wonder)

The cruise ship is to leave New York December 27 and arrive in Alexandria, Egypt on December 31, 1999, just in time for its passengers to celebrate New Years 2000 at Giza at the Great Pyramid of Cheops. The last surviving monument of the Seven Wonders of the Ancient World has drawn paleontologists, architects, anthropologists, and members of the Millennium Society of Washington DC.

Ron, a paleontologist, has been married less than two years to Jody and is taking her on a belated honeymoon trip by cruise ship to Egypt. It's a lifelong dream for Ron and a sentimental journey for Jody. They have spent the last of their wedding money on the trip to join the celebration at the Great Pyramid and welcome the new millennium.

The ship undergoes rough seas and is late. There won't be time to move the passengers to Giza in time for New Years. Jody and Ron are distraught. After all the planning and spending, it looks as if they will miss the big event.

As the ship nears the coast, the seas become even more volatile, heaving and swelling until, with one big swoop, the ship is carried by tidal wave straight across the Nile delta and deposited at the foot of the Great Pyramid of Cheops.

Round Trip — To the Circus (Magic)

Mary Holly was born in the year 1900. Halfway through life and halfway through the century, Mary decided to live to see the next century. She wants to celebrate making it to an even 100 with a return trip home, to a Milwaukee suburb. Struck down with severe health problems in the 1960s, she renews her vigor (along with numerous hippies) in the 1970s, with yoga and healthy living. She manages a new lease on life in the 1980s. The aging Mary finally learns to kick back and enjoy life in the 1990s.

But inactivity and cynicism begin to wear down her spirit. Is there reason to live any longer? With the '90s becoming kinky (weird), is there reason to look ahead with any kind of hope for the next century?

The trip to Milwaukee is strenuous, but old Mary perks up when she arrives in her old home town. "That used to be a vacant lot where we played ball. Over there is where we used to have a skating rink in winter with an old shed for a warming house. And that's the old schoolhouse, now an antique store. I kissed my first sweetheart out behind…"

The newspapers pick up the story and come to Mary's hotel room for an interview. In the course of the interview, Mary realizes what a full life both she and the century had — surviving wars, depressions, assassinations, boxing matches, floods, fires, and earthquakes; new discoveries in medicine, the auto and airplane, computers, radio and television, movies, and circuses. Maybe life is all a struggle, along with calamity, wonder, and circus magic.

At the conclusion of the interview, a reporter asks why she chose to return to Milwaukee for the New Century's celebration.

"I'm not sure," begins the old woman. "I knew I wanted to celebrate somewhere special. I've always loved Milwaukee, maybe because we lived here for so many years. I decided on the trip about five years ago while attending a family reunion.

At the airport, I overheard some people talking about getting reservations at that fancy New York hotel. One guy said it would be difficult since there already was a waiting list. I recall that one guy said he could get their names on the reservation list by breaking into the computer. What makes people so hotsy totsy fired up to get into some ritzy place?"

"Human nature, ma'am, would be my only guess."

The old woman leans her head back a moment and lets *human nature* sink in. "I got to thinking that if I lived this long, I wanted to do something special to welcome in the 2000s. It was five years ago that I booked a reservation at that fancy New York hotel… oh dear, I forgot to cancel it…. Oh well, they won't miss me. It was after that my son called to tell me he had booked his company into the Seattle

Space Needle for the New Century celebration. 'It's still five years away,' I told him, but he said he barely made it. The Space Needle and other high-up places also had waiting lists."

Mary closes her eyes again and wanders off, coming back with, "Amazing. That was when Jody met Ron, remember?" she asks to no one in particular. "Oh, you don't know them. Jody is my granddaughter. Ron is the guy from the Smithsonian, a paleontologist or something; they're married now. Safe on a cruise in the Mediterranean." She sits up and shifts her small body as if to stand. The interviewer rises too and helps Mary Holly to her feet. "But you didn't come to hear about my family and all their plans for tonight."

ARTEMIS

"That's her, over there, the one with the bow and arrow."

"Wouldn't you know she'd bring it with her."

"Why do you suppose she does?"

"Goddess, I don't know. Must be a hunting thing. Maybe she thinks she's Cupid or something."

"I heard she runs about on moonlight nights waving that thing. Must be a family problem."

The women gossiped on about the woman they knew as Artemis. "Who would ever call a child Ar-te-mis?"

"Well, she sometimes calls herself Diana. I saw her Social Security card once. Yep. It's Diana all right."

The woman known to friends as Artemis and to Social Security as Diana had nearly forgotten her arrows that morning when she left her condo. Grabbing the bow had become second nature, but lately she'd begun to forget the arrows. And, she had walked all the way to the parking garage before she realized she hadn't brought her quiver.

"I must be getting senile," she muttered under her breath as she returned to her front door. She was fumbling in her pocket for the key when she heard a bump from inside her apartment. She froze, not daring to move, waiting to hear another sound.

She stood that way for some time, her arm in mid-air, key in hand, her ears sniffing the air for another sound. Then, there it was, a definite sound of scraping. She had no doubt; someone was inside her apartment.

Very very slowly, she extended her arm and inserted the key in the lock, very very slowly. She squinched her eyes and pursed her mouth as she very carefully used both hands to turn the tumbler, ever so gently, very slowly.

There. The lock is open. Now for the door handle. Wonder how they got in. I thought the back door was always locked. Did I forget and leave it open last night after I took out the trash? Who could it be? What do they want?

The door now ajar, Diana pushed it aside as quietly as she had opened the lock.

Okay. I'm inside. Now where… there… thank goddess, I left the arrows next to the hallway mirror. I'll just…

The woman leaned over so she wouldn't take any more steps than were needed and wrapped her fingers around the quiver. She lifted it, inches at a time so the shifting bundle wouldn't alert whoever was inside. She slowly hung the strap across her shoulder and reached inside for an arrow.

One more minute and I'll be ready, she thought. *Then we'll see what's going on here.*

As swiftly as she had previously been slow, Artemis pushed aside the door and leaped through it, dashing into the kitchen, where she had heard the sounds. The arrow poised on the string, her bow aimed directly at the intruder, Diana shouted, "Stop!" half scaring a man who stood unrolling his tools on the butcher block.

The man's hands flew into the air, his head cowered, anticipating an arrow through his chest. "Don't shoot," he feebly cried. "Don't shoot!"

"Why not?" Artemis countered. "Why the Hades not?"

"I'm the plumber," the man managed to squeak. "I'm the frickin' plumber you asked the manager to fix your dishwasher."

Artemis paused a moment, her arm tiring from the tension on the bowstring.

"Please put that down," the man whimpered.

"Uh, oh," Artemis stammered. "Guess I forgot. How'd you get in? And why didn't you come when I'm home?"

"Well, the manager gave me the master key for the back door. I just wanted to get the thing fixed and get out of here. I called out when I came in, but there was no answer. Please put down the bow." The plumber then blinked and widened his eyes. *Bow? She's carrying a bow!*

Artemis very precisely held her aim, then let loose the arrow. It pierced the plumber's shirt just under the pocket. He never had a chance. In the next few moments, his frightened look softened to a smile and he introduced himself sweetly.

"Hi, my name is Dan and I'm here to fix your dishwasher. But hey, how about we take a few minutes and go out for a cup of coffee?"

That Day...

Charlie Prinz loved to draw. The sketchbook he always carried had become an extension of his heart that flowed through his fingers to the pen in his hand onto the paper.

That day...

July hadn't a thought in her head most of the time. She seemed to move from one place to the next, directed by some remote power, controlled from someplace near the stars. She studied science and history and social economics, yet the music in her head soothed her face and shone in her glorious eyes.

That day...

We'll get to that day, but first you need to know a bit about these two. They had never met until that day in Paris; both of them were foreigners. Charles never replaced his English with French enough to speak fluently; July knew only the English she learned in French schools. July came from a family that never hurt for money; Charles' family had long ago sent him off to find his fortune among the other Beatniks of the '60s. He had committed the family sin of wanting to bypass the family medical practice and live life for himself.

Charles had been lured to Paris by its artists — and its hidden wealth. He knew how to find them both. Daytimes he hung out in one of the cafés near the campus where rich kids idled away daylight hours awaiting the night. At night he settled his sketchbook and pens in a café near the embassies that cuddled within their walls the rich diplomats and their well-paid staffs of foreigners.

The young man sat quietly in a corner, sometimes behind a potted tree, or sheltered from view by a counter. As he sipped a coffee or glass of Bordeaux, he watched for "the" face, the face that exuded sentiment, reflected grief, sought comfort, bypassing the beautiful faces that showed little emotion. He never had to wait long. He learned the facility of foreigners to wear their emotions on their faces.

At night, near the embassies, he caught on paper the turmoil of a world gone mad, of the problems of state, of upheaval in families. He carefully and quickly sketched, first a draft, then a finished portrait. He had to work fast, since he had to complete the portrait to coincide with the dessert wine and cigar. Oh yes, he almost always chose to draw the males in the room. To do otherwise might earn him a fisticuff; he learned that lesson early.

He had chosen a beauteous subject one evening, soon after his arrival in Paris. She bore a stately pair of shoulders, atop which was held a head, high, as if balancing a crown. While her beauty would seem apparent to a passerby, the artist immediately saw hidden pain, as if her face where holding back the injustices of centuries. He had drawn quickly that night, eager to finish his portrait (of a queen on the throne). He caught just right her haughtiness that protected the pale cheeks and sad eyes.

The dinner finished without her speaking a word. She occasionally nodded her head or shook back a waiter, but the others in the party, all men, completely ignored her. As a bland dessert of dark fruit of some kind was served, the Vergine Soleras was poured. Charles gathered up his portrait and approached the table. He smiled, muttered a brief *bon soir*, and placed the portrait in front of the lady.

She nearly smiled before the old man to her left grabbed the portrait and glared at the artist. His string of epithets was protected by a language Charles had never heard. He wanted to believe the older man was delighted with the attention to… his wife? Or perhaps an old lover? He soon realized he had committed an error in selecting this model.

The man reached for the Marsala bottle and was about to knock it over Charles' head, but the young man sprinted off to his corner. What crime had he committed? Had he insulted the wife… or the man himself? Was his drawing that bad? To this day, he cannot answer those questions. But he quickly deduced that women, at night, among a group of men, were not profitable subjects.

Daytimes, while not as profitable, usually proved more fun. Among the youth at the cafés near the Sorbonne, he felt more comfortable. On occasion, he ran into other artists practicing their sketches as they sipped lattes. Charles could see they weren't as polished as his work, and he often struck up small talk with them, as much as he could with his limited French.

"Bon jour," he would begin. Then, pointing at the other artist's drawing, "Bien. Tres bien." That was about it. Sometimes the artist bought him a cappuccino and sometimes Charles was rewarded with a blank look that said, "What the hell do you know about art? Go away."

Daytimes, in cafés near embassy schools, Charles could draw the faces of young women to his heart's delight. He almost never drew the beautiful faces, but chose those with character peeking out, the sad, mournful, deluded faces that described lives of empty wealth, uncaring parents, friends that weren't really friends, and loneliness. Oh yes, the loneliness had become Charles best drawings.

Like the Friday before Easter when most of the students had rushed off to holiday beaches in the Sud de France or mountain cabins in the Urals. He spied a young woman pouring over her schoolbooks, attempting to look as if she was concentrating. Her face held downcast eyes, heavy eyebrows, a slightly off-center nose, and a mouth turned down at the corners, but lips apart, appearing to read aloud.

Charles knew immediately that her clothes came from the trendy shops on the Champs Elysee and her hair had been done that morning. Not that it was coiffed like Marie Antoinette, but her classy haircut needed constant trimming, which it received. He sketched a rough draft, watching for the moment her eyes would leave the pages and look up. When they did, just for a moment, he saw in them a pain that reached deep into her soul — and he caught it with his pen.

He took longer than usual with this portrait. By the time he finished, he held it at arm's length and softly sighed. He had caught her. He had captured her sorrow, her feelings of being left behind, her misery of being alone.

He gathered up his work and walked over to stand across the table from her.

She looked up. He gestured to sit down. "Sil vous plait?" She gazed at him for a moment before she nodded. His smile was not returned, but he noticed her face relax as if she was seeing the sun peek out from behind a cloud.

"Bon jour." Her courtesy exposed her lack of French. But Charles didn't want to talk. He opened his sketchbook and pulled out his drawing, placing it atop the book she was reading. She stared at herself in pen and ink. Her head tilted as she continued to study the work intently. After a moment, she looked at Charles and the sun came out fully as she smiled a smile that told him he had saved her. "Moi? Bon." She reached for her purse. "Combien?"

Charles shrugged. He never placed a price on his work. In this case, that smile she flashed was worth it all. However, he opened his hands as if to say, "whatever you feel is right."

She hastily pulled out a few large franc notes and placed them before him. Charles stood up, tucking the notes discreetly into his pocket, smiled back at her, bowed deeply, turned, and left the café. She didn't notice. She sat holding the portrait before her, still smiling.

So you can see what kind of fellow he was. Charles was an artist, commanding skill with pen and ink as well as with people. His days in Paris, drawing, watching people, drawing, sometimes eating, and drinking coffee or wine, and drawing, were pleasant. Charles was a happy young man.

And July? July was always happy. She wandered Paris streets as if she owned them, which she could have if her mother's trust would cover the bill. It wasn't quite that much, but it kept July and her mother in a comfortable apartment, fed them truffles and champagne, and gave July a freedom to become whatever she wanted. The only difficulty lay in the fact that July didn't know what she wanted.

July never had to work; her mother's trust provided all she needed. It was that *wanting* thing that kept her guessing. Once she wanted to become a flight attendant and fly all over the world; that lasted for just two days of the training. She wanted to try nursing; she didn't get past the first blood test. She even considered clerking in one of those delicious dress shops on the Rue de St. Germaine, but clerking was for the poor. And July was not poor.

July's mother had inherited a great deal of money from her husband when he died. That was the story that July heard. In truth, July's mother had taken money that didn't belong to her, and fled to Paris to spend it.

July's mother — her name was Lotus, or at least the Indonesian equivalent of that lovely flower — grew up in India, and had to leave her family when it grew too large to feed her. She, as did many of her school friends, wandered about the waterfront looking for visiting sailors to make happy. She earned enough over a few months to move to higher ground, the hotel area where rich foreigners paid higher rates for her services.

It was there she met the charming Japanese envoy who had been sent to India to establish connections that would aid them in their approaching war. He became a regular client over several months and Lotus was becoming financially secure by the time her opportunity presented itself.

Bit by bit, Lotus had figured out her client's business, and she had sweet-talked him with questions about how he managed such a sensitive arrangement with his Indian counterparts. A sucker for praise and eager to please his darling companion, he told her more than he should have.

More importantly, he showed her the suitcase full of yens that amounted to a sweet life somewhere for someone. He actually hinted that the two of them might take advantage of their budding possibilities and run off somewhere with that suitcase.

Lotus, impatient for a better life, couldn't wait. Already pregnant with the baby that would become July, Lotus padded her growing belly with wads of yen, turned some of them into British pounds, and caught a plane to Paris. There she converted her suitcase full of yens into British pounds and secured them in investments in three British banks before quietly settling into a life of pleasure on her own terms. She learned to speak fluent French, and melted into the background to observe a dreadful war.

Her greatest pleasure was raising July. She pampered the child, giving her everything that her own childhood had been denied. She lived on the outskirts of Paris to avoid contact with German soldiers. She was rich enough to feed herself and July by means of the black market. And when the war ended, she quickly gathered up their belongings and moved to a delightful home in a burgeoning suburb.

July grew into young womanhood, following Lotus to museums and art galleries to learn about magnificent art. As Europe recovered from war, they traveled more often, taking brief jaunts to Italy and Spain, once to Norway, but quickly returning to their cottage, feeling the pull of "home". Lotus was becoming a Parisian dowager and enjoying her status as Madame with a capital "M".

Now a young woman approaching thirty, July felt an emptiness in her life. Certainly, it was filled with things. But what was the purpose of it all? Not that July ever asked that question of herself. Rather, she took things as they came to her, one day at a time. Learning to speak almost perfect English was her only achievement to date, and that just happened as part of her schooling. French schools were turning global.

Once a week she took the Metro into the city center, leaving the limo at home and walking through the noisy streets. She always caught a shiver as she climbed the steps that led into the Rue de St. Germaine and came upon the crowds of ordinary people busily avoiding bumping into her as she stood still a moment to take it all in. Who were these people? And where were they going in such a hurry? This is Paris, people. Slow down and enjoy your city.

Her weekly trip included a stop at the hair stylist who kept her black shiny hair under control. For a time, when she was in high school, she clipped it short to see how she looked. Her mother was aghast at the atrocity of chopping off her lovely hair that had not seen a scissors, ever. But Lotus's tears were more effusive than July's. There was a kind of freedom in shaking her head without the long tresses flopping about.

That weekly trip also included lunch at a very elegant dining room, where July could try out her new French twist, see the effect of her lovely hair on the other women in the room. Most of the French ladies had never seen such lustrous black hair. Was the girl Japanese? Chinese? Her eyes were slightly tilted, but enough to be a real Asian?

It was July's smile that turned the women back to their vegetable crudite and bef champignone. The young woman strode through the room, looked back over their heads, smiled a gracious nod to everyone and no one, and sat down, as any queen entering the dining hall would have done.

Not that July was a snob. She simply enjoyed the looks on the faces of her audience as she played the part. Most other times, she enjoyed a quiet omelet supreme at a local café, surrounded by tourists in summer and clerks on lunch breaks in the winter. She repeated the performance for late lunches, enjoying a bowl of French onion soup (Lotus would have sneered) and a lovely combination of French eggs and French vegetables, with French bread.

For July knew nothing of anything that was not French. She felt as French as Joan d'Arc or President DeGaulle or Edith Piaf. No wait, Edith was American, but she sounded French and she made French music. July liked that.

July had a song in her heart, a melody that played itself over and over as she walked the Paris streets, mingling with the Paris people. While not the national anthem, it stirred her heart and sent her to symphony concerts with Lotus.

Yet, the music by the great orchestras did not match the music in her soul. It wasn't the same. Something deep inside her was contorting her soul, seeking release. She wasn't sure exactly what it was, but she wanted to find out.

That day. You're wondering about that day. To remind you: Charlie Prinz loved to draw. The sketchbook he carried always had become an extension of his heart that flowed through his fingers to the pen in his hand into the paper. That day, his fingers itched with expectation.

That day…

July was rolling thoughts around in her head. She constantly roamed from place to place, following… what, she didn't know. Something was missing; something was shouting for her attention, and she couldn't hear.

That day was not her usual trip to central Paris. That day, July was drawn to the musical studies halls at the Sorbonne. She had heard about the way early musicians had learned to temper their musical souls through studying even earlier musicians. Why not? She had time; she had money; she had music in her being. Why not study and nudge out that music from the depths?

The morning of that day, July had risen early, hopped on the Metro to the Sorbonne and sought out the music department. A helpful young man near the entrance had guided her to the dean, a pleasant old gentleman who looked a bit like a bust of Bach that July had seen at the Louvre. They talked for a half hour about music, about July's expectations and hopes, and about classes that would help her reach them.

The dean handed her brochures and reports and fall schedules and papers that he helpfully piled into a folder. At length, he rose, extended his hand, and directed her to a counselor who would arrange a class schedule for her.

July shook his hand, thanked him for his time, and headed out the door, bypassing both the young guide and the referred counselor. She'd figure this out herself. The glow of her face had returned to her glorious eyes.

That's why she sought out the nearest café, ordered a café au lait, and found a table where she could spread out her stash. She couldn't help but know this was a life-changing day. She, July, was going to release her music. She just wasn't sure how that was going to happen.

Yes, her life would change, and in ways she never could have guessed.

Charles had decided that summer was no time to waste on work. The sun was already beating down on the Paris streets as he walked leisurely through the Jardin de Luxembourg. He paused to watch the children at their end of the park before strolling under the plane trees, past the ice cream seller setting up his stand, to the giant fountain surrounded by gardens.

He found a bench and watched people for more than an hour, never lifting his pen to his sketchbook.

Where was he going? Why wasn't he at some hospital directing a roomful of physicians? Why had he chosen the life of art? It had all seemed his destiny when he was a teenager, but now he was approaching adulthood… no wait, he already had reached that milestone, he was getting old. My god, he'd be thirty soon. Had he sealed his fate by leaving home at such a young age? Had he chosen wrong?

No, he hadn't been wrong. It was the thing he had to do… then.

But now? What about now? Could he spend his entire life sketching faces that had become repetitive to him? Sure he made a decent living, but he was tiring of the faces. So many looked alike to him now. Perhaps he could find a garret, learn about oils, and get down to some real art work. Perhaps he could even… take an art class? At his age? With his talent? Out… of… the… question!

Charles Prinz sat facing the fountain, listening to the sweet giggles and soft words from the couple two benches over. Where was his love? Was art enough for him? Could he imagine himself on that bench with that woman... no, not today. Perhaps someday. Someday he'd find someone to share his life with, but she'd have to be an artist.

So where does that leave me? His mind circled and flew over the treetops like the crows that chided him from the air. Dead end. Charles, you've hit a dead end, he decided. Maybe taking off the day from work was not a good idea.

That day Charles rose heavily from his fountain-side bench and walked slowly toward the nearby café. He entered and sat idly at a table before realizing he had to order from the counter. He rose slowly, leaving his sketchbook behind, and walked to the counter. He had to wait in line to order his coffee and madelaine before he returned to his table.

"Pardon," he intoned in his most ardent French. "Por quoi?" he asked. What are you doing with my sketchbook? The question was posed to the young woman who had picked it up and was paging through.

She began a string of French phrases he couldn't comprehend before realizing he wasn't understanding. She tried English on a hunch. "This is yours?"

"Uh, yes. You speak English. Are you English?"

"No, I am French, but we learn it in school."

"You sound British."

"Well, uh, that *is* English, isn't it?"

Charles placed his coffee on the table and asked again. "What are you doing?"

"Oh, these sketches are yours. I was admiring your work. You're an artist."

"Yes." Charles couldn't find more words. He was staring into the most beautiful pair of black eyes he had ever seen, surrounded by one of the most beautiful faces he had ever seen. And it wasn't just the slightly Asian look, or the creamy skin that glowed, or the makeup that enhanced it. He was seeing something in a beautiful face he had never seen before — life, desire, hope, plans, meaning, significance, importance, consequence. Something was happening with this young woman that was... important.

"My name is July, spelled like the month but pronounced with an 'e'. I saw your sketchbook and was curious about what is in such a book. So you sell your work? Are you a successful artist?"

So began that long conversation that went on for more time than most conversations between close friends.

Charles and July sat facing each other, mostly forgetting to sip their coffees, talking about art and work and childhoods and music and families or lack of them and futures and pasts and forevers. Radiance glowed around that table in the corner of a little French café that lovely summer afternoon.

Listening to the sweet music of their hearts and watching the tender thoughts of their minds and tasting the refilled cups of the past and sensing the perfect timing of the future and touching lives of two people as they gently touched each others fingers — all of this defined the boundaries of all the arts into one sunny afternoon in Paris, that day.

ON THE RIVER

On the river in the wintertime lay a memory of a young boy and a young girl who braved the dark of midnight and the cold of New Years Eve to encounter the wind and their dreams.

She slipped out of her house just as the neighborhood church clock struck midnight — the beginning of a brand new year. With her new white figure skates slung over her shoulder and snow boots warming her feet, she trudged alternately through snowdrifts and shoveled sidewalks down to the edge of the river. The snow falling lightly and blowing from the tall fir trees reflected what little light shone down from nearby streetlamps. Approaching the shelter of the fir trees, she caught first sight of a figure out on the ice, appearing much like a small sailboat skimming in front of the blustery wind.

She sat on the big log to remove her boots, noticing the other pair of boots. *Just like him,* she whispered to the trees. *Always showing up at the wrong time.* While she had looked forward to trying out her new skates by herself, she felt oddly safe knowing that he was nearby. She laced up her skates hurriedly, then clomped down the wooden board toward the ice.

"What's she doing here?" he said to nobody in the middle of the frozen river. Although he had looked forward to trying out his new hockey skates by himself, he felt cheered to have company. He lowered his "sail" and headed toward shore.

"Hi," she called. "I thought that was you."

"Yeah, it's me," he returned. "Thought I'd try out my new skates."

"I got new ones too."

"Bet they're not good old hockey skates like mine."

"Course not — they're beautiful white figure skates. 'Bout time too — my old ones were all worn out. Much as Dad tried, he couldn't get the runners as sharp as these."

"C'mon out — the ice is perfect. I had to brush off some snow, but the ice is smooth."

"The cracking isn't dangerous?"

"Course not, girl. Just says it's getting colder and deeper. Bet you could drive a truck on it right now."

"Well okay — here I come."

She skated onto the ice, spreading her arms suddenly for balance as she felt the sharpness of the new blades. "Ooh, these skates are great!"

"I think you're a good figure skater — for a kid girl anyway."

"Not a kid girl!"

"Yes you are!"

"Then you're a kid boy!"

"Am not! I'll be thirteen next year… I mean this year. Hey, Happy New Year!"

"Thanks. What're you doing with that broom?"

"It holds my sail. See? I stick the end through the sleeves of my jacket and I have a sail." Just then a blast of cold air gave him a sendoff down the river. She laughed so hard she lost her balance and took a header. Quickly, so he wouldn't see her spill, she got back to her feet and brushed the snow off her snowpants.

If you were hovering near the river that cold blustery night, you'd have noticed how two youngsters began to notice each other in new ways. You'd have seen how he flew past her, jacket sailing in the wind, a wide smile on his face and hope in his heart that he wouldn't hit a rough patch of ice and fall. And you'd have seen her find her balance and twirl and glide over the ice in a performance for the stars, and him, that equaled the Olympics.

Will you look at that! Some fifty years have frittered away, and there are the same two people walkin' up to the edge of the river on a snowy holiday night. Sure, it's a bit earlier in the evening than before, but they're still hauling their ice skates over their shoulders. This time he helps her lace up her skates; she helps him move his fragile old legs to stand up on his skates. Together they approach the crackling of the night ice, arms about each other. Once on the ice, he opens his jacket and lets the wind take him out to the middle where he drifts along with the wind. She stays near shore, renewing her figure-eights and floating swans.

Two happy people… on the river of ice.

FEAR AND TREMBLING

(IN 300 WORDS OR LESS)

What scares me? you ask. What fills me with fear? Not the plain stuff, for sure, that you're likely to hear. It isn't invasion, bombs, flood, or typhoon. If I have to get up without light, it's the gloom. Unable to see, that's a fright, and it hits when I'm moving about in the night.

What's even worse, the thing that gives eyes the glazies is driving the freeways, avoiding the crazies with cell phones and food filling their hands as they drive, oblivious to steering demands.

And rushing, my dears, is what drives me to drink. Speed sends me flying right over the brink. While drinking, of course, and (or while) driving is manic, the thought always drives me right into a panic.

Something else that scares me, I hesitate to say, but I'll tell you truly, is drug use today. I'm not talking aspirin, although that's where it starts, but all the stuff that TV aims at our hearts. The promises told of beauty and truth, dressed in purple and pink pills, to expect happiness, youth.

We're filling our bodies, heads and souls — don't scoff — with stuff to benumb us and turn our brains off.

But for terror that's sheer, are those expectations galore that tell us we can live forever and more. We're fervently told "to stay young" is a goal. It takes up our time and fills up the soul.

"What scares me the *most*?" you ask, not the dark, drugs, or disease, or speeding with cell phones, or guns, heights, or bees. It's not even retirement that turns my blood cold; it's passing a mirror and seeing I'm old!

One Sentence Story

(in 500 words or less)

The little girl, her dark hair flowing in the breeze and her blue eyes closed in contemplation, sits on the backyard swing, barely moving her legs to keep it swaying back and forth listlessly as she strains to keep from listening to the angry sounds of the grownups coming from the half-open kitchen window just a few yards away, accusatory words flying recklessly from her much-loved father and returned in similar abrasive tones from the child's adored mother, as they argue about who is to take their only daughter to the zoo for a weekend outing, a regular weekly occurrence that the child looks forward to with mixed feelings of hope and fear, for in the past three months or so these weekends have brought incessant combat that frightens the child, barely five years old, not yet in school, which she is looking forward to because she is the kind of child who keeps looking ahead, who wonders if she will ever enjoy another day at the zoo, or the park, or the mall, or movies with her parents, either together or separately, since they seemingly are unable to agree whether or not they want to spend time with the child, or so it appears to her, a youngster who has become perceptive to her surroundings since she learned to read, partly as amusement and partly in order to distract herself from this part in her life that causes her to listen weekly to the ongoing critical dissention between her parents, the couple who once laughed and held her hands as the three of them danced their way to the park, the loving parents who taught her how to plant seeds in the backyard and watch them grow into sunflowers, who fed her books to read and beautiful things to look at, who inundated her with squishy toys to play with and ripe strawberries to paint her little mouth red, and who read make-believe stories to her every night as she dozed off in her all-pink-and-white canopy bed in her all-pink-and-white bedroom, to dream of fairy princesses and fuzzy animals who loved her and helped her forget those long ago times, the times that should be long forgotten (since they most likely will not occur again) but which remain foremost in the head of a beautiful little girl with long dark hair who sits impassively on a swing in her backyard, her head down, her eyes closed, and her ears attempting to filter out the rude sounds of her parents, as she watches the shifting ground beneath her indifferently, and as she drags her toes in the sand and listens only for a song in her head that she may never hear again.

SECTION III

AH! CHILDHOOD

Childhood is a time for joy and play without concern for safety and wellbeing. However, many children do not experience that period of life joyously; many live in fear, hunger, danger, and loneliness.

The writings in this section reflect children of all kinds: those living life with abandon and those living life with abandonment. More and more adults are learning about children living in outwardly happy, safe homes, but who are suffering ills ranging from loneliness to violence.

My childhood is a joy to remember. Even during the years of the Great Depression, when I felt as if we were "poor". I now realize we were among the lucky ones. My father had a good job (teacher and principal), and my mother introduced her children to the creativity in life. Believe it or not, I have my kindergarten scrapbook, compiled in 1934-35 (in much the same way I am now compiling this book).

That kindergarten scrapbook contains my earliest writing, even though it's mostly my name or the identity of the picture I drew. The yellowed pages contain animated figures, created with the help of very imaginative teachers. Crepe paper was the material of choice for costumes and decorations; shiny paper was for drawing and painting; colored construction paper was for building; and crayons — Crayolas — were the rage.

We lived next to a river at one point, where I learned about fish and drinking water and flooding, mostly from my father. He was the kind of man who answers simple questions with very complete answers.

My favorite memory of that home was its proximity to a sauerkraut factory. As harvest progressed, large horse-drawn wagons passed our house, riding over pitted roads. The jolting wagons often dislodged freshly picked heads of cabbage, which rolled along the rutted road until collected by us children. We'd tear off and discard the outer leaves, then dig into a delicious snack of fresh cabbage. I still taste those leaves when I eat cabbage that way today (except I don't have to find a bumpy road to provide them).

Other memories include tap dancing lessons, which never "took" with my less-than-talented toes; building snow igloos over the side tracks of the train station across the street; the friendly old folks who welcomed us to play around the station; the steam trains that shifted around the station in the middle of the night, their creaky metal parts sometimes keeping us awake (until we got so used to the sound, we seldom woke up).

Good old days? Maybe not so much. We had to keep cats to control the varmints that loved the river; we didn't have freezers or automatic anythings; my mother worked hard every day keeping us in clean clothes and tummy filling food. Still, my dad found time to take me fishing, where we lolled under a tree on the river bank until I caught a giant fish — that sometimes measured as much as six inches. Yum! It tasted good at suppertime.

My best friend in those days was a girl named Joyce who lived kitty-corner from our house in the apartment over her dad's cheese factory. Do you wonder where I developed my love of all things dairy?

Joyce's mother ran a beauty parlor and showed me how to curl my very straight hair. My friend and I shared the burden of having younger sisters; we also shared the limelight during dance performances — except that Joyce added gymnastics to her steps, which I could never get the hang of. Ah, those summer days practicing our "routines" on the lawn at our house.

The stories in this section tell about all kinds of children and all kinds of childhoods. Perhaps that's because I find other children's stories more intriguing than my own. Enjoy them.

BABIES

Babies are for loving, giving our love to — or are they? Could babies be for giving us love?

Toodles was the first baby Ellie tried to love. She was a doll, a small rubbery, soft doll, usually without clothes. The toddler held her by one arm or leg, not your acceptable maternal trait; she was only this many (three fingers). Still, she loved her Toodles.

A few years later, there was Louise, an intellectual friend. Both Ellie and Louise were older and wiser than Toodles. Louise was named for Louisa Mae Alcott, an author recently discovered by Ellie. The two became constant companions, taking long walks and holding long talks together.

The next time Ellie thought about babies was when she was 15. She had a vivid dream about having a baby, all her own. She named him Jared Eric Davis and called him by his initials, JED. That may have been her first maternal stirrings, or a teen-age romantic idea of what love was all about. That baby was someone she could love safely without the commitment of a real live person. Ellie counted his birthdays, one month, two months, six months, until several months slipped by without wishing this imaginary baby a Happy Birthday. JED remained in her dreams, waking and sleeping, but he lived as vividly as a teenager could imagine.

Ellie's next baby was unnamed, unborn, unwanted. Afterwards, she longed to have known if it was a boy or girl. But this baby wasn't with her long enough to have even a soul, much less a body. It died before it was big enough for a soul — a miscarriage at three months, three months after the "altercation". She shouldn't have been pregnant, not in those times when women wore white gloves and hats and didn't even use the P-word aloud. (Her properly-married sisters were referred to as p.g., spoken in whispers.)

Ellie didn't believe she was p.g. then. She didn't want to be. Even decades later, she found it difficult to believe that thing happened to her. Still, that first pregnancy was the manifestation of a sexual attack that shouldn't have happened, and wouldn't have happened if she hadn't accepted a date with the wrong person. The first time a real part of the young woman joined with a real part of someone else — and it died.

Ellie prayed no one would find out. They never did, until she confessed to her doctor years later when her first child was on the way. Panicked, she was afraid that the miscarriage would affect her legal baby who had been awaited for a long time.

Her first real live pink cuddly baby was a daughter. Even then, Ellie felt a bit like she was a Toodles. Although she didn't carry her with one arm, she didn't feel particularly maternal either. She seemed somewhat unreal, given all the other babies she had.

Ellie stopped thinking of JED and that first pregnancy as child after child was born in the sterile birthing room of a sterile hospital. "I showed him, didn't I?" Ellie smiled at her family. "Six babies in all! I showed them!"

Perhaps babies are for loving. Perhaps they are more for loving, for providing the love we don't find in other places. A helpless baby needs someone to cling to, belong to. Babies are for loving — and giving love back.

MEMORIES OF CHILDHOOD

Memories of childhood usually are pleasant images, nostalgic. Most likely there are myths of your childhood that, when you look at them closely, were not as you remembered.

Swinging under the apple tree. Naptime alone, shades drawn, sounds of carpenters pounding, motor boats on the river. Being fed in a highchair. Car rides. Digging worms to go fishing with Dad. Waiting for Daddy to come home. Birthday party. Dance lessons. Tricycle riding when there was only a short sidewalk.

Childhood at School

First day of school: feelings of being tossed out of your home, rejected by your parents, sent away. Sit still and be quiet! Don't talk back. Don't talk. Don't even whisper. Don't shout. Don't daydream; pay attention. Stand up and recite. Do as you're told. Don't imagine. Don't stand up to protect yourself. Don't tell…! Stand in line. Don't fidget (don't feel your own energy). Don't express yourself! Don't laugh, giggle or smile. Wipe that smile off your face. Stay within the lines.

Don't play. Don't enjoy yourself. Don't wiggle. There, there, you're not hurt. Don't hurt! Don't cry! Watch teacher's face. Don't be wrong. Don't ask questions. Don't get sick. Don't feel bad, sad, glad, or mad. Don't feel! Sit up straight. Stand straight. Don't touch. Don't be nosy (curious or questioning). Don't be scared. Don't be tardy. Don't get sleepy. Stay in line. Don't hang back. Participate. Play nice. Play with classmates. Don't leave the school grounds. Don't leave the room. Don't leave your seat. Wait for the bell. Don't be absent (you missed that lesson). Pay attention. Listen. Look, see. Draw this. Sing that. Play this. Paint that. Stay within the lines. Stay in line. Stay lined up, like waiting for a firing squad. Stay tense. Don't relax. Try to relax, loosen up.

Now snap to! Obey orders, follow directions, write your name in the upper righthand/lefthand corner; keep one-inch margins; leave a space between lines. Hold the pen like this. Draw flowing letters. Write clearly. Show your work. Don't put in needless lines. Pronounce each syllable. Speak up! Read slowly. Don't dawdle. Keep up. Stay in step. Altogether now... hands over head, to your side, bend over. Stretch upwards; reach for the sky. Wiggle your fingers. Hold your partner's hand. Buddies stay together. Don't run. Don't rush your work. Complete your work on time. Hand in assignments. Pass your paper forward. Pass your paper backwards. Check your neighbor's answers. Don't cheat.

Present your book report. Don't fidget. Look up once in a while. Don't tell the ending. Don't give a short book report. Don't make your report too long. Don't count your words. Count your words. Write exactly 100 words. Bring a pet to class. Don't bring animals to school. Feed the turtle. Don't feed the turtle. Don't play with the turtle. Feed the goldfish. Don't feed...

Learn words by heart. Don't guess. Sound out each syllable. Learn the rules. Play by the rules. Read by the rules. Do math by the rules. Draw by the rules. Sing by the rules. Write by the rules. Don't break the rules.

Keep your desk in order. Come prepared. Hand in neat papers. Do your homework. Work in the classroom. Don't waste time. Take your time. Watch your time. Plan your time. Be neat. Clean up after yourself. Keep your hands clean. Wash your hands. Don't play with your food. Don't exchange lunches. Eat all your food.

Go outside to play. Walk around the schoolyard. Share the swings. Don't hog the swings. Don't throw the ball too hard. Don't hold onto the ball. Play nice. Take turns. Let everyone play. Choose up sides. Don't choose the wimp. Choose the popular ones first. Leave the rejects until last. Be a leader. Take control. Be a good follower. Join the team. Join in the game. Don't be left out. Don't cry if you're not chosen. Don't play alone. Don't walk alone. Don't sit alone. Don't sit. Stay moving. Play, damn it, have fun! Come in when the bell rings. Don't delay. Run. Don't run. Don't sweat.

Settle down. Get your mind back to work. Don't look out the window. Don't watch the teacher. Pay attention. Don't let your mind wander. Don't wonder. Don't dream. For god's sake, don't fall asleep. Step up to the board. Don't guess. Don't make mistakes. Don't look silly. Don't clown. Don't be a comedian. Stay calm. Think! You know how, you know the answer. Search your brain. Do it this way. Remember. Do it again. Keep on trying one more time. Again! Write 100 times... Go to the board. Go to your seat. It's your turn; it's not your turn. If you're so smart... Don't be smug. Don't be so sure of yourself. You think you're so smart, show the class. Tell the class how! Let the class in on your secret. Don't whisper. Don't pass notes.

Take the test. Don't look at each other. Don't look at your neighbor's paper. Eyes forward. Look at the teacher. Look at your own work. Look at yourself! Write clearly. Print. Leave white spaces. Fill the paper. Use correct grammar. Don't forget the correct punctuation. Don't guess. Fill in all the spaces; don't waste time; complete all the answers. Do the easy ones first. Use extra paper. Use scratch paper for your work. Don't use other paper. Put all your work on the page. Show all your work. Don't be nervous. Keep alert. Don't be careless. Make every answer count. If you don't know, leave it blank and come back to it later. Use only pen and ink. Use only pencil. No erasures. If you change your mind, erase neatly. Cross out the old. Keep your paper neat. Keep your answers short. Answer each question completely.

Don't pass notes; don't get caught passing notes; don't pass notes for anyone, even if they ask. Don't lie when you're caught. Take the assignment, write the damn essay, and don't talk back. Never talk back to the teacher, even when she calls you a thief. Keep your mouth S-H-U-T!

Don't rush. Don't drag your feet. Move along. No loitering in the hall. No walking in the hallway between classes. Use a pass. Go to the office. Don't go to the principal with every little problem. Don't call home. Don't bring toys to school. Don't bring parents to school uninvited. Tell your parents to come anytime. Make your parents come to teacher conferences. Don't be a baby. Your parents can't help you now. You're dismissed. Stay after school. Go right home after school. Clean up the schoolyard. Clean up the chalkboard. Sit up straight in your seat and don't move for a half hour.

You're a disgrace to your family. You're a disgrace to your classmates. You're a disgrace to your teacher. You should be ashamed of yourself. You're no good to anyone. You're a mess. You're a disappointment to the world, your school, everyone. No one will like you. You will never make anything of yourself. You'll never be able to hold a job. You're a failure. Whatever will become of you?

Childhood at Home (Soft)

Don't touch. Don't fuss. Don't dawdle. Don't play with your food. Don't put everything in your mouth. Don't play with yourself. Don't throw your toys. Throw the ball. Don't cry. Don't fall down. Don't sit there. Don't stand that way. Walk here. Don't stare. Don't pout. Don't embarrass your parents. Look at your mother. Don't yell. Don't run in the house. Go outside and play. Don't run away. Stay near the house. Stay in the yard.

Speak up. Tell Mother what hurts. Don't whine. Find someone to play with. Find a toy to play with. Find something to do by yourself on such a nice day. Learn to amuse yourself.

Feed yourself. Eat everything on your plate. Try some new food. Don't eat too much. Eat this and you'll feel better. Don't talk back. Don't sass your parent. Mind your mouth. Mind your manners. Say please and thank you. Give me that. What's behind your back? You're a sneak. Don't do things behind your parents' back.

Always tell the truth. Don't tell. Don't snitch. Don't tell family secrets. Don't be rude. Smile and be happy. Don't get excited. Keep quiet. Go away. Don't leave the house. Be independent. Stay with your parents. Don't take chances. Don't risk. You'll never amount to much if you don't try.

Trust your parents. Don't trust anyone. Don't question your parents. Question everyone and everything. Don't trust your own eyes. Don't take no for an answer. Obey the rules. Do as your parents tell you. Sit in the chair and be still. You'll be told when you can get up. Sit up straight. Don't talk under your breath. Learn to take orders. When you're told to do something, do it. Don't do anything before you're told. Don't do everything anyone tells you to do.

Don't lie in bed. Get up when you're called. Don't wake up your parents. Don't mope. Be pleasant in the morning. Must you talk so much? Eat your breakfast. Drink all your milk. Don't be late. Don't forget your lunchbox, your books, your sweater. Don't leave without kissing your parents. Take care of your sister. Don't run. Don't miss your bus. Don't look back. Don't be late for school. Don't be late coming home after school.

Don't yell when you enter the house. Don't forget to close the door. Don't bang the door. Did you wipe your feet? Don't stomp. Don't make so much noise. Change your clothes. Do your homework. Pick up your cap. Hang up your coat. Clean up your room. Do your chores. Don't forget your homework. Don't ask your parents for help. If you need help, just ask your Dad. Don't tease your sister. Stop fighting. Settle down; your father will be home soon. Settle down, your mother is worn out from a long day. Settle down, or you'll be sent to live with your grandmother.

Get cleaned up for supper. Don't come to the table with dirty hands. Don't fight at the table. Don't talk with your mouth full. Don't bore your parents with your day's activities. Don't chatter. What did you do all day? Sit down when you eat. Don't eat in front of the TV. Don't turn on the TV until your homework is done, your chores are finished, and your hands are clean. How long since you took a bath? Change your clothes, Wash your hair. Don't think about wearing earrings until you're old enough. Don't wear makeup until you're old enough.

You're not old enough! You're too old for that. Don't be a baby. Don't think you're a grownup yet. There'll be plenty of time when you're a grownup. Why do you act like a child? Why can't you act more like an adult? You're old enough to know better. You should be old enough to do that right. Here's how to do that. Do it the way you're told. Don't experiment. Don't try things your way. Don't try things you don't know about. Don't try. You never try anything new. Why don't you just try this… once? You'll never learn until you try.

You just don't know how to do anything. You're a disappointment. You're stupid. Any other kid knows how to do this; you should. Don't try this on your own. Follow the directions. Take lessons. Learn before you try this on your own. Don't be so damned independent.

You'll never amount to anything. Lean on your parents; depend on them. Pay attention to your parents and plan to follow their direction. Why can't you leave your mother alone? Why can't you do anything by yourself? Are you going to depend on your parents all your life? They won't always be around for you.

Clean your room. Straighten up your life. Don't smoke. Don't drink. Don't take drugs. Don't notice that your parents (family members) smoke, drink, gobble sleeping pills and aspirin. Don't eat too much. Eat everything you're served. No one will ever want to marry you. You're a failure. Whatever will become of you?

Don't need anyone. Don't depend on anyone. Go it alone. Be strong. Only the strong survive. Don't show weakness. Don't be sensitive. Don't be insensitive. Don't be afraid to show your real self. Understand your parents. Accept their faults. They'll never understand you, nor accept your faults. Feel your own strength, not theirs. Feel your own weakness; it isn't theirs. Cling to your parents. Honor your mother and your father. Then forget everything they told you — and get the hell out and live your own life!

Childhood at Home (Hard)

Shut up! X God, why were you born? X Don't you do
anything but cry? X Don't cry. X Don't breathe. X Don't
just lie there. X Don't look at me. X Don't touch me. X Get
out of here; nobody wants you. X Leave me alone. X

You're a curse from god. X You're a chain around my
neck. X Don't follow me. X Don't eat if you don't want to;
maybe you'll die. X I wish you were never born. X Shut
your mouth. X You're despicable. X Don't you dare wet
your pants. X

You're a mess. X You're stupid. X You're no good. X
You depress me. X You're a mistake, a fucking mistake. X
You shouldn't have been born. X You ruined my life. X

You're a dirty pest, an insect, a bug. X Get away from
me. X Nobody likes you and everybody hates you. X You'll
never learn. X You're a rotten shame to the world. X You
can't do anything right. X Crawl into your hole and die. X
Nobody will miss you. X You don't deserve anything. X
You can't do anything right. X

If it weren't for you… X You're always in the way. X
You do everything wrong. X You're a reminder of all that is
evil. X You'll never be anything. X You're not worth
dragging around. X You're too damn clumsy. X Damn you!
X Damn your life! X You're a curse. X You're a miserable
excuse for a child. X

Get your freaking hands off me. X Shame on you. X
Stop crying. X You're such a damn cry-baby. X Don't you
understand? You're not wanted. X Nobody wants you. X
Get out of the way. X You're scum. X You remind me of
slime, dirt. X You are worthless. X You're shit. X You're a
miserable sniveling worm. X

Get the hell away from me. X You better mind. X Don't
you open your goddamn face to me. X Shut your filthy

mouth. X You're nothing. X I'll teach you a thing or two. X Go to your room and never come out. X Stay out of my fuckin' way. X Get lost. X Go away. X Why don't you die? X Why were you ever born? X

[X = slap, hit, smack — or punch with hand, fist, stick, board, toy, rolled up newspaper, arm, TV remote, cooking pot, furniture, beer bottle…]

LITTLE GREEN APPLES

Summer spends a few days in northern Wisconsin — usually in late July or August. It's always been like that, even back in the 1930s. The sun shines mercilessly during those summery days, sometimes to the chagrin of the hay threshers and the women cooking over the old wood stoves. The kitchen feels even hotter than usual as the women make jokes about "ladies who never sweat; they glow."

Children love it, the heat — my sister and I always do. We find a shady spot near the water pump house where we can make mud pies and cakes, taking moments to grab a sip of cold, icy cold well water.

The best times are the afternoons, luncheon dishes put away, animals fed and watered, children fed and… well, it is quiet time. On the hottest days, Mother leads us out to the orchard where we find apples on the trees, beginning to look like apples except they are not red. But we find our treasures on the ground, where the thunderstorm a couple nights earlier shook them loose.

Gingerly, Mother shows us how to find smooth green apples and check them for worm holes or "bad places". Then we pop them into her basket. When we have as many as we can carry, we hike back to the house, keeping as much in the shade of the apple trees as we can, pausing occasionally to pick up still another "perfect green apple".

In the cool of the kitchen (the wood stove fire has died down), Mother washes the apples in cold water from the well and places them in a bowl on the table — that lovely great kitchen table that serves as dining room, entertainment center, psychology couch, and social parlor — and invites us to help ourselves.

My little sister has to have Mother cut her apple into small pieces, but I dig my teeth into the taut skin and lick the peeling. Then I dip the damp area into the salt dish and stick the apple back into my mouth. Ohmmm! I can taste the tart, slight sourness, compensated with salt. And my mouth still waters.

COUSIN LULABELLE

My first lesson in sex education was taught to me by my cousin, Lulabelle. Her real name was Loretta, but we all had kiddish names for each other. Her big sister was Genna; my little sister was Mimi; and I was Budgette or just Budge. Our mothers loved to point out the birth order, with two years difference between each of us.

At the time of this lesson, Genna was 12; Lulabelle was 10; I was 8; and Mimi was 6 (the 2-4-6-8 girls). My cousins lived in River Falls and my family was preparing to move to Milwaukee. We moved around a lot while my dad was working up in the school system from teacher to principal.

Our families got together on winter holidays, usually New Years, and during the summer school vacation, usually the Fourth of July. My father and Lulabelle's mother were siblings who, we speculated, were very close during their own childhoods. I loved Aunt Ethel for her infectious laugh, her musical voice, and her loving arms. She also baked up a holiday storm!

I particularly looked forward to spending New Years holidays with Aunt Ethel and my cousins. My Uncle Sammie was a Norwegian (not Scandinavian, but Norse!) who loved food from the old country (he taught me how to make and drink hot black coffee). Aunt Ethel was a fabulous cook who created Christmas delicacies to die for. Especially the rosettes she made of very fine pastry and sugar. She kept them in the cool upstairs bedroom where my sister and I slept. You can imagine how many of those creations disappeared overnight!

But let us get back to my sex education. It was during the summer I was eight, when our family lived in River Falls so that my dad could update his college degree. We stayed with the grandfather we all shared, but I spent much of my time with my cousins. We walked in those days, and Lulabelle's house was only a few blocks from Grandpa's.

On one of those warm summer days, Lu and I took our week's allowance and walked towards the town center. We especially liked to visit the ice cream shop where they served malted milks for ten cents that melted all the way to your stomach. It was on one of those trips to town that Lu spotted her.

"See that lady?" she whispered. She didn't point, but nodded in the direction of a young woman.

"The one with the navy blue dress?"

"Yes." Lu paused for effect before she took hold of my shoulder and pulled my ear towards her mouth and said very quietly, "Budgette, she's going to have a baby."

I had never thought of such a thing before and asked blandly, "How do you know?"

My wise cousin spoke very slowly. "Look at her tummy. It's big. There's a baby in there."

"What?" My cousin played the role to the hilt while I ate up every word. My disbelief must have amused her.

"True. God's truth. She's going to have a baby."

"But how will it get out?" That worried me for some time, although Lu tried to explain it to me.

She spoke slowly and seriously. "When it's big enough, she will go to the doctor and he'll take it out."

My mind whirled. I didn't want to show my ignorance in such matters, but I couldn't help asking, "How can that be?"

"I'm not sure of how they do it, but that's what Genna said."

Questions filled my head for a few more years. How did the baby get in there? How exactly would it get out? Didn't it hurt? What did the doctor have to do with it all? It took many more years before I realized that was how I too started life.

Loretta and I were close as cousins. She was my guru in all things grownup as we loped along through those childhood years. She had answers for everything, and I soaked them up. As little girls, we played dress-up in her mother's clothes closet. Loretta loved hats. And she introduced me to makeup, painting my face until I looked bee-oo-tee-ful (in her words).

During winter visits, she took me ice skating at the high school outdoor rink where she pointed out the boys she liked. In summer, we went swimming at the park pool where she pointed out the same boys. Some of them splashed water on us and followed us home, but she never gave them a tumble. Oh, my cousin Loretta was so cool.

As we grew into the teen years, Loretta took up with a guy from out of town. In those days it was very adventuresome to date boys from other towns. I guess when you've grown up with boys who push you down on the ice rink and splash water on you in the swimming pool, you want to look elsewhere for dates.

Anyway, she told me, in her Lulabelle whisper, about this boy she met who was shy and dashing at the same time. He sounded just right for her. I was about to graduate from high school and Lu was already in the world. I don't remember if she had a job somewhere, but I would guess she did. "He's a dreamboat," she kept telling me. "His name is George and he lives on a farm near Prescott, and... I... think... I love him."

"Oh, then this is serious."

"Gosh yes. Serious." She looked at me in astonishment and added, "I think I'm going to marry him. I'm going to be a farmer's wife." She couldn't have looked more sure of herself or happier.

When the announcement came, I wasn't surprised. George and Loretta seemed so right for each other. The best part followed when Loretta asked me to be her maid of honor at the wedding. It was a beautiful wedding.

As this newly married couple rode off into the sunset, I just knew they'd have a long and happy life. Strangely enough, I got entangled with my own life and never had the opportunity to see Loretta "with child", although she gave birth to five of them. I suppose, after all those years, she figured out how that process worked and didn't mind a bit!

PEPIN

As a kid, I always thought "Pepin" was a funny name for a town in the middle of the country. Somewhere about the fourth or fifth grade, I learned the derivation: Pepin was King of the Franks in the 8th century; as such he established papal authority in that part of western Europe. He was also known as Pepin the Short — which I liked better because it was funny — like the town.

The town of Pepin is located on the Wisconsin side of the Mississippi River, on the banks of Lake Pepin, which is probably the first wide spot in the river after leaving Lake Itasca, its source near Minneapolis. Lake Pepin freezes over every winter with ice so thick it can support cars, and (a long time ago) my figure skating attempts. In the summer, it sometimes warms up enough for swimming. I don't recall anyone ever daring to swim across the one mile to Bay City, Minnesota, but I'm sure someone did.

The reason I know so much about Pepin is that some of my relatives live there. My mother's sister Aunt Mic, her husband, and their two sons spent most of their lives there — and grandchildren still roam those quiet town streets (no longer dusty, as I recalled them in summer, or crunchy with snow in winter). My family spent most Christmases with my aunt, uncle, and cousins, until the year my father died. After that, Mother visited her sister's family a few times, and I spent weekends there when I was attending a nearby college.

Altogether, Pepin holds some of the best moments of my life. It's where I learned to ride a bicycle — an old beat-up thing with a bare chain that caught my pants regularly, causing terribly embarrassing moments when I had to remove my slacks, outdoors!

Pepin is also where I learned about community. Most of the town knows everybody in it and is related to many of them. Nobody locked their doors or cars then. Kids walked wherever they needed to go: to the two-block downtown area that harbored a movie house that changed its movies every two weeks, a general store, and a one-pump gas station; or to the lake to go swimming or boating; or to a nearby creek to fish for bass; or to hike up the bluffs that served as backdrop to the town. We thought they were mountains and bragged about walking all the way to the top (a mere three miles, but a long trek to a 10-year-old).

Somewhere at the foot of one of those bluffs was a Girl Scout camp that I attended a few times. As a wannabe writer, I always kept journals of special events, such as trips or camp, certain birthdays, a winter holiday or two, and a fishing trip with my younger cousin. [Why would a 12-year-old girl accompany a nine-year-old boy to the fishing creek? Because she didn't know how to fish!]

All of those childhood adventures took place a half-century ago. Why am I remembering them now? (I ask a lot of questions, don't I?)

Answer: Something happened yesterday that took me back to Pepin, complete with view from the top of the bluff, the feeling of a warm breeze on my sweaty young body, and the smell of summer. I even recalled the bologna sandwiches my aunt had prepared for us, and the taste of chocolate milk from a thermos bottle.

I'm still not sure if all those memories were part of my dreams or if they were just lying in wait for something to stir them into reality. What I saw was the valley below the bluff as a backdrop to three little girls who I was interviewing. They appeared to be 10, 13, and 16 years old. Who were they? Why were they with us on top of the bluff? And why now?

This morning, I realized it had something to do with those specific times in my life. So I dug out my journals from Girl Scout camp, and out dropped some letters that I had sent to my family. I won't say they were yellowed, but they sure felt brittle as I carefully unfolded the pages one by one. And there they were! Among the other notes of special moments in a young girl's life were the following letters. I marveled at the changes in temperament and thinking that were reflected in each successive letter.

The first letter was a nasty one from my first year at camp. The year I was ten: *Mindy says she doesn't like me because I come from the city. She thinks I'm stuck-up.*

The second letter showed a mellower me, a young girl beginning to grow up and very full of herself: *I like to think my cousins like to have us visit, but I hear them talking and know they think I'm a bother. If only they knew how talented I am, playing the violin and piano, and they don't play anything except baseball.*

By the time I was 16, I had found some direction in my life and had developed a budding values system. Read this one and notice how grownup a teenager feels and how circumspect I seemed as I psyched out my friends: *My cousin is planning to join the Navy and will probably go off to war. Why do we have to have wars? I hope he will know what to do and not feel out of place. I don't think he's ever been away from Pepin.*

Other memories of Pepin: fishing in a creek bordered with wild flowers, making vague attempts at casting, catching a good-sized fish, followed by a dip in the muddy water. Swimming off the jetty that was built of stones to form deep water for boats, the water cold but fun. My uncle's hand-made boat that sat for so many years unassembled in the garage while he worked on it.

Holiday food from my aunt's kitchen: dishes of candy, fresh-baked bread, venison (and learning to skin and preserve deer meat), home-canned vegetables, vanilla ice cream (churned amid piles of snow and served with strawberries preserved from the previous summer), dill pickles from a barrel buried next to the garage, sauerkraut from a barrel in the basement, comic books in the attic, boys' games, hemlock and weeping willow trees in the backyard, peanut butter from a different kind of jar, Christmas cookies.

At Christmas, the evening service at the large Methodist church in a town named for a papist! Christmas carols I had never heard before, riding around in my uncle's car to look at Christmas lights, staying awake to see Santa, the sound of bells on sleighs at night, wading through snow up to my waist, learning to ski, and figure skating at midnight.

The drive to and from Pepin, counting the crossing of the six low culverts and the one big bridge; staying at Grandma Lilly's home next door, the smell of rubber stair mats at the door, her spotless home, and a featherbed. Learning that my cousins had "other relatives" not related to me, their girl cousin, giggles at the movies, and summer picnics in the town park with family and friends.

But oh, the quiet of Pepin! An occasional passing car or sleigh or wagon. Parking in a snowdrift. The run to be first inside to greet my aunt. The house and its evolution: first, only a kitchen, dining/living room, bedroom, and wash room (no plumbing at first, then faucets only); the finishing of attic rooms for the boys. Other additions, a living room across the front of the house, and later a screened-in porch at the back. Tar-papered exterior for many years before being covered with gleaming white shingles.

And all of it, every minute of the time spent in Pepin, was full of love — family love.

FLYING IN A SWING /1

"Oh how I love to go up in a swing, up in a swing so high…", words of Robert Louis Stevenson rang in my ears as I enjoyed my swing. Even though we moved a lot when I was a child, my father always found a tree to attach a swing to — a comfy wooden seat, held to the tree with a strong rope. I called them "barn ropes" because they often were similar to those used in winches to hoist hay to the hay loft and to pull machinery around the farm.

I love to fly in my swing while I dream of soaring over the heads of people, housetops, trees, fly off into the sky and enjoy adventures. Some day I'll break loose of these ropes that hold my swing to the apple tree. I'll just sail off over the river, past the school, and out… there… wherever and whatever is out there.

Someday I'll be a grownup lady and wear high heels and long dresses and wonderful hats with feathers and jewels and… then what will I do? I never got past the *dressing-up and flying-off* stage as far as dreaming of my future. I never saw me as a librarian, or a teacher, or a hairdresser (my only professional role models), or even as a mother. It just didn't seem like a possibility, none of it. No one ever told me I'd grow up to be a woman.

If they had, I'd have been prepared to deal with my body, to acknowledge that I had a woman's body that did womanly things. I'd have been able to understand why I was treated differently from boys, how I wasn't supposed to do some things that boys did. I'd have learned much earlier to ride a bicycle. I'd have learned much earlier what was under the hood of an automobile. I'd have spent more time hiking in the hills, building campfires, staying in the woods all night alone, playing baseball, but mostly bike riding. I ached to ride a bicycle, but girls didn't do that. Even after I convinced my father that some bicycles were made for girls with special construction, I wasn't allowed to have one. I managed to ride one only by sneaking away to my cousin's and riding his.

If I had been coached on becoming a woman, I'd have known how to talk to boys. In grade school they were bullies, wild and uncontrollable. They didn't sit. They always ran and shouted. They didn't know how to talk quietly. I didn't like them.

By the time I was in 5th grade they had become mysteries — untouchable mysteries. I watched them from a distance, thought about them when they weren't around, dissolved if one spoke to me. And I never, never, never spoke to one of them if I didn't have to.

I enjoyed wearing dresses in the workplace. But at the first opportunity (when fashion allowed it) I jumped into slacks and stayed there. I was miserable those times when I had to "dress up". I came to hate high heels and frills, as heartily as I had admired them as a child.

What happened between that little girl who couldn't wait to grow into patent leather pumps and wispy skirts and the grown woman who lives in jeans and T-shirts?

What happened indeed! That little girl learned that boys have all the fun, do the exciting things, reap the benefits, receive the honors, gain opportunities that girls don't. Boys grow up to be men who go out and work in the big world, make money and spend it, control the household, the country, the rules, the wealth, the past and the future. Men drive the cars, fly the airplanes, sit on the judge's bench, run schools (although they don't teach), govern the city, state, and country, fight wars, travel to Asia and Africa and South America, make plans and carry them out. Women don't.

Why on earth would a young girl want to grow up to wear high heels and frilly dresses?

FLYING IN A SWING /2

Oh how I love to go up in a swing

Up in a swing so high

Up to the top of the trees

Up to the top of the sky

Swinging, sitting on the solid wooden board, holding onto the thick rough rope, I pump myself back and forth until I am soaring almost to the top of the limb where the rope is tied. Once in motion I can rest, pause, look around, search for the horizon. There it is, beyond the trees across the river, dim in the spring light, hazy behind the black tree skeletons. Where it leads I can only imagine, which I don't because the nearer sights compel my attention.

I see the river running swiftly with the spring thaw, swelling and overflowing its shores, enjoying warm breezes. Robins return to nest in the limbs above my head. They deposit pale turquoise hope in their newly formed homes and sing amid the fragrant apple blossoms.

I swing until my head touches the blossoms. Idly, I wonder if anyone ever swings so high they circle the branch. Would I fall out if I did? or just hold on and return rightside up?

Push me — push the swing hard. I'm big enough. I'm not a baby. I can swing high. Don't hold me back — push me. Let me do it. Let me go. Let me fly high, even to risk circling and falling back. I long to fly — higher. Higher. I want to be a special person, renowned in my field. I want a career, a career that my mother never had. I shall be famous; even the robins will know me.

Preparation and education are important. That is basic, fundamental, like learning to hold onto the ropes. Perhaps that's what *learning the ropes* is all about. I must do it well so that what follows is spectacular.

Those ropes are strong. As hard as I tug, as hard as I pump, as much as I swing my legs and pull against the ropes, the swing goes only so high and no further. Just once, can I summon the courage to try to go full circle around that limb?

The strong ropes remain secured to the limb, keeping my radius constant, keeping me tied to the tree, never to see beyond the blossoms — as the robins do when they are freed from the nest at last.

What am I missing? What is it that holds these ropes (and me) to the tree? Have I missed something important? Is there a gap in my thinking? my plans? my performance?

Oh, how I love to go up in the swing, up in the swing so high. It will never be high enough. I can never escape over the tree top, swing around the limb full circle, and soar away past the river over the trees seeking the horizon.

Why? The answer comes like a sharp knife scratching the skin and opening a deep wound.

I am the one who has chosen to swing. I am the one holding onto the ropes. I am the one who decided to sample the joys of flying while holding tight to the tree. All the while I watched and envied the robins as they came and went, adding new life each year, soaring upward through the fragrant tree, living each day to its fullest, living as they were meant to live, no more, no less.

The catch is that I never realized how I was meant to live, never realized that soaring and holding on are not possible at the same time. I chose holding on rather than risk the soaring. I chose it. No one tied me to the swing. No one required me to stay with it. No one coerced me into holding on. No one, except me. While I waited for someone to push me higher, push me away, push me into free flight, I held on.

Is it too late to try to fly alone? Too late to let go and soar with the robins? New robins come along, generations away from the birds I knew when I first climbed aboard the swing. Can I keep up with them now that I have become used to swinging in half-circles? Is it too late to try?

Turquoise shell fragments remain behind to mix with blossom petals that flutter to the ground like confetti. I remain, swinging on the limb of the tree, pink and turquoise confetti beneath me, green leaves and blue sky overhead. Ropes hold me to a circle that is never complete, just part of a circle, back and forth, back and forth, never to know the *beyond* of free flight.

Children's Games?

Blind Man's Buff

Blind Man's Buff is a children's game I remember playing with gusto. I felt I had a guy's sixth sense that helped me see without using my eyes. I would place the blindfold carefully over my eyes, making sure that no light got past. Then, listening to the shuffling and the muffled laughter, I'd grope around the room, running recklessly and bumping into furniture. Never mind if my shins were bruised.

What was important was finding someone to grab, someone I could know wasn't as smart as I was. I have to admit I didn't try too hard, because if I caught someone I'd have to remove the blindfold and the game would be over. I found much more excitement in darting around the room, bumping into whatever, groping for…

What did I grope for? What do I grope for? Am I still playing Blind Man's Buff? That feeling of groping in the darkness, reaching out, trying to grab hold of... what?

That feeling still pursues me. I can't identify it more than that, a groping for something.

Left Brain kicks in: do I want a relationship? a career? a family? a purpose? sanity? safety? sense? sensitivity? What do I want, old boy?

How often since those days have I felt this recurring sense of reaching out for something and finding only air, space, nothingness?

In college I longed for a field of interest, something to catch my attention and hold it. I flailed through innocuous courses, past insensitive teachers, into my own recognition of what is important. And it didn't match anything that schools could offer. I groped for purpose, touched emptiness and quit.

Relationships have been a joke. Over and over I sought and found just the right woman for me. Carolyn was perfect, or so I thought. She didn't. I wanted so much to help her forget the mistreatment her father had caused, wanted to ease her back into feeling a relationship with someone who cared for her. I couldn't.

Then Andrea came along. She needed me as I wanted to be needed. We worked together and became friends before her husband picked up and left her to make out for herself and their small child. Andrea needed someone to support her, a place to stay, a shoulder to cry on, help with caring for her child. I fit the bill; I was there; I was needed. For a time. Then she found her own strength and returned to living by herself.

Somewhere in that past was Barbara. Barbara was perhaps the strongest love of my life. I guess I loved her from the time we met during 6th grade camp. We rode bicycles together, horsed around on the playground, walked in the woods holding hands. We had a strong relationship going until Barb discovered drugs. We both experimented with reefers in high school "just for the fun of it", but Barb opted to continue the fun. I didn't. It finally came down to my issuing an ultimatum — drugs or me. She chose drugs. I've always regretted issuing that ultimatum.

Relationships haven't been my strong suit. Every time I find someone who needs me, someone I can touch with my blindfold on, I grab. Then they wriggle out of my arms and I am flailing again at the air, groping for someone else to need me.

The same way I groped for a career. I thought I discovered my talents, my direction in life. I put everything I had into the venture — money, energy, time. I even started my own business for a while, offering carpentry services to little old ladies. They loved me, paid me well, and patted me on the back for doing a good job. Why couldn't I stick with it? Why couldn't I keep up the pace? They needed me.

Like Blindman's Bluff, the ones who want to be caught are the ones who need me. They aren't the ones I'm looking for. Who wants to catch someone who wants to be caught?

Moving into mid-life (approaching 30), I'm thinking about a family. My own has long disappeared, gone their own way. It's time I had a family of my own doing. But how and where do I look?

I place the blindfold carefully over my eyes. I reach out toward the muffled sounds, then run wildly about, trying to catch someone, hoping that I don't. Because if I catch someone, I'll know she is someone who wants to be caught. And where's the challenge with that?

What is this game I'm playing? Groping, reaching out, trying to catch something that I don't want, frantically beating the air to find... what? When I touch someone, I hold on tightly, perhaps too tightly, trying to make them depend on me. I grasp and strangle until I lose them. I fail with that which I most want to keep, or do I?

What is this game called Blind Man's Bluff? and why the hell am I playing it?

Button, Button...

Button, button, who's got the button? is a game played with children. (It works extremely well if the children are waiting for something and need to remain in place, preferably sitting down in a circle.) One person is It. That person, It, places a button between their hands so others can't see it. Then It moves from child to child around the circle and pretends to drop the button into another person's cupped hands. At some point (or not) It decides to drop the button, passing it on to another (who will soon become It). When It gets tired of walking around, a selected person is offered an opportunity to guess who has the button.

Button, button, who's got the button?

With children, it's a great pleaser. They wait expectantly, excited about the prospect of being chosen. Will the button mysteriously appear in my hands this time? Will I be the keeper of the secret? What will I do if I receive the button? Can I look innocent while I harbor the treasure between my palms? The guesser has the most fun, trying to uncover the guilty person, psyche out the facial expressions, read the body language that so often provides all the clues that are needed. Can I stare down the suspects and reveal the secret-holder?

The person with the most to gain in this game, however, is It. It can choose anyone they wish to give their power to. It can select the next person to be It! That is heady stuff.

Monday. I feel subdued, lazy after a long weekend doing not much. I probably should have done some baking for the holidays, or cleaned out the den so I can work at home comfortably, or taken Jake to the movies, or taken some time just for myself, shopping or exercising. But instead, I frittered away the weekend doing laundry, reading back issues of the newspapers, reading magazines, and watching television. And here it is — Monday.

Who will I give the button to today? Let's see. How about Mr. Benson? He hasn't had it for a while. Okay, Mr. Benson, you're going to get the button; you're It.

"Good morning, Mr. Benson. Did I understand you had a report to get out before the 10th? I thought so. Drop it on my desk this morning, and I'll see you get it right away. What? You didn't like the last work I did for you? Yes, I know I can't spell worth a darn, but I use the spell-check on the computer. Yes, I realize I am just the receptionist and I shouldn't be doing this work for the executives. But I want so much to do something more. I feel so inadequate. I want you to like me… but, Mr. Benson, you always say I am doing a good job. I just want to…"

Button, button, who's got the button?

Tuesday. Who gets the button today? I feel really great. I got out of bed early today and had a good breakfast, got all green lights on the drive to work. I feel terrific! I think I'll select Marie to give the button to today. You're It, Marie.

"Marie, how's it going? We haven't had lunch together for a long time, how about today? What? I never told Nancy any such thing. I know you and Nancy talk about me behind my back. Of course, I know it…. Well, no, I haven't heard you, but I know you do. I feel it whenever I walk by and you're talking. I know you don't like me…."

Now I really feel rotten. How can she ruin my day like that. She is so insensitive.

Button, button, who's got the button?

Wednesday. Middle of the week blues. Can I make it to the weekend? Perhaps I ought to begin making plans. This seems like a good day to give the button to Tony. I'll call him during my break. We can go see the new movie he said he wanted to see. Better yet, I'll rent some videos and we can stay home and chew on popcorn and snuggle. You're going to be It today, Tony.

"Hi, Tony…. Yes, it's me. I was thinking about you this morning…. I know, you said we should have some time to ourselves, but I don't need more time. I'm renting videos and you can come over Saturday and… no, I realize I didn't ask, I just assumed… you do, you made plans? Tony, I thought we… but, you said we… okay, so I didn't think, I just miss you and want you to… Tony, please, Tony…"

How can he be so cruel? How can he hurt me so much? He's a real bastard to make me hurt so much. Maybe I should dump him, send him on his way. I really hate him.

Button, button, who's got the button?

Thursday. Long weekend ahead, nothing to do. I'm feeling miserable. Depressed. I don't want to spend the weekend eating, and alone at that. Mom. I'll give the button to her.

"Mom, I haven't seen you in a few days. How are you? Have you moved that sofa into your bedroom yet? I thought maybe I could come over this weekend and help you, if you want. Maybe we could even take in a movie, or something…. You are? Alone or with somebody? I could go with you if you… oh, he's driving. Well, if you want to go off with him rather than spend some time with your daughter, I guess… No, Mother, I'm not laying on a guilt trip, at least not any more than you've done to me… oh, I didn't mean… I don't want you to… oh, Mom, I'm so miserable. I'm so alone. I hate my job; I don't have a social life; I hate the way I look; I have no friends. I need you. Oh, Mom… Mom… don't say that. Don't do that to me, I…"

Button, button, who's got the button?

Friday. Who can I give the button to today? Maybe this is the time I need to go shopping, do something nice for myself. Nobody else seems to want to. Yeah, I'll splurge. I'll get a new outfit, some new perfume, a gourmet take-out meal. I'll feast alone tonight, but I'll feast.

There! Two new suits for work, a new dress for going out, two pairs of shoes, and an ounce of real French perfume. Now for the gourmet take-out and I can go home and… oh dear, how much did I spend? I can't afford all this. My poor credit cards are so overloaded, I'll never catch up. And this food will probably add six more pounds that I don't need. Why do I let those people talk me into buying all this stuff. I'll have to take it back on Monday.

Button, button, who's got the button?

Saturday. Is there no one I can give the button to who will deserve it, who will treat me the way I want to be treated? Who can I trust to take the button and use the power to help me out? Who will accept the button quietly, inconspicuously, discreetly, and keep their mouth shut?

I want to give the button to someone who will accept it as a gift from me. I want them to give it back to me in trust, friendship, honesty, support, encouragement. I want someone who will use the power on my behalf, someone who will… I want someone who will treat me the way I want to be treated, who will be nice to me. Who could that be?

Could I be looking in the wrong direction? Should I be holding onto this button myself. Oh my god, I've been trying to give away my power, to place my welfare in the hands of someone else, some ones who don't give a damn about me, as much as I wish or think that they should. Truth: There's no one who can give me what I want. Only me. I'm the only one who can.

Button, button, who's got the button?

Me!

Hide and Seek

Who has more fun playing Hide and Seek? The hider? or the seeker? The hider has to find a place out of sight and remain a part of the game. If you aren't hidden well enough, you might be caught right away, and the game wouldn't be much fun. If you're hidden too well, you may not be discovered; no one can find you, and you'll be alone.

The best way to hide is to find a place where you are concealed, but where you can watch the proceedings. You can see how the seeker progresses, who gets caught, when it's time to be discovered.

The seeker has to know all the good hiding places, has to know who prefers what kind of concealment. Who prefers trees and bushes? Who finds boxes and hidden corners? Who camouflages themselves in brush, flattening themselves on the ground? Who likes to climb trees and peer out from the leaves?

The seeker also needs patience. And good ears. Some hide just long to be caught right away, can't stand the thought of being somewhere without someone knowing where they are. They make noise automatically, as naturally as singing out their location. The patience is needed for the hiders who secure themselves away and dare anyone to find them. They don't want to be found and can hold up a good game for hours while everyone searches — the seeker and all the others who have turned themselves in.

There's always somebody who does that. Runs off, goes home, takes a trip to the store, dashes away without telling anyone. After all the others have come in, the seeker calls "Ole, ole, alls in free," but there's always one who doesn't show up.

Once, long ago, the gang would give up and go home themselves, figuring out that the no-show had taken off alone. Today, kids must look and look until the person is accounted for. These are dangerous times, and who knows but that someone, some dastardly menacing criminal, hasn't carried off their friend.

Hide and Seek may not be a game for these times. It may be a relic of the past, doomed to be shelved until people can play again, at least can play fairly, honestly.

The problem with playing Hide and Seek now is that it's played without physical hiding. Today, players hide themselves, who they really are, behind facades, not easily penetrated. They are in full view physically, but they hide their personages, their characters, their real selves.

Some choose to hide periodically, from time to time, from certain people, but they usually choose places where they can be discovered easily. They don't want to hide, not for long, not from everyone. So they pretend and provide scads of clues to anyone taking the time to play Seeker.

Seekers are becoming scarcities too. Fewer and fewer people take the time to seek out others, to look for the hiders, even the ones who leave bread-crumb hints lying around. The seekers use more energy to look for themselves. Never mind taking the time to look for others.

Too bad about those hiders who choose now to take off and hide permanently. Nobody seems to care anymore about finding them.

Hop Scotch

Do you remember the smell of warm mud in the spring when the snow has nearly disappeared and the moist earth reappears from beneath its winter mantle? Something about the first warm breezes of spring melts the last of the snow, exposes the ground with its nascent grass and makes it smell sweet and full of life to catch the senses.

Oh, the joys of re-examining the outdoors after being cooped up all winter, re-igniting friendships and fights and playing together with neighbor children who haven't been seen without snowsuits for months. The memories rush back at the smell of mud once again.

Hop scotch was the big game, played as soon as the snow cleared the cement. Damp mud and growing grass confined us to the cement ways where we scratched the hop scotch outlines and searched for markers.

Rita always chose a flat stone. She believed the stone was heavy and could be depended upon to stay put where she tossed it. Maggie selected a lighter weight piece she called petrified wood. It was probably a flat stone, but she pointed to the markings that gave it a woody appearance.

As for me, I chose a ruby, a dark maroon stone, shiny and smooth and sparkling. I found it along the river when the stream was low one summer. It had been worn smooth by lapping waves that removed the sharp glass edge. It probably came from a bottle of something Mother would call sinful, the devil's brew. I could tell from the dark color, like Daddy's scotch bottles.

Like my scotch bottles. There, just like that one. Toss one of those on the rocks down by the river, wait a few years for the water to do its work and you'd have a great ruby marker for hop scotch.

I can look right through the glass of this bottle and see those carefree days like they were yesterday. Rita and Maggie and I playing hop scotch, still wearing the baggy cotton stockings from winter wardrobes, wearing heavy sweaters or jackets, but free from snow pants and boots as long as we "stayed on the cement".

How we longed for those precious spring days. How we longed for the end of winter, the end of the confinement, the discomfort, the heaviness of winter clothing. How we reveled in the freedom of warm breezes, the promise of warmer breezes, the freshness of a world being uncovered as the snow melted.

How we enjoyed the competitive fun of hop scotch, the challenge to our winter-cramped muscles to stay within the lines, teeter on one leg and manage the turns at the end of the outline. I still can see the numbers scrawled on the sidewalk, sometimes in chalk (if we could sneak a piece out of the school room), sometimes scratched with a rock that uncovered lighter cement under the worn surface. The numbers appeared wavy through the glass. Perhaps the light isn't as clear now as it was then.

Rita, bossy Rita, always laying down the rules, always calling the fouls, keeping our feet honestly within the lines. Rita is a judge now, still laying down the rules.

Maggie, who giggled constantly and always saw the brighter side of anything, kept us from killing each other when a close call was made, when a disagreement arose. Maggie stays true to form and now referees a houseful of her own children, keeping them out of each other's hair, keeping the peace.

Me? I found the rest of the scotch bottle that once was my marker. I very carefully glued it back together, keeping all the pieces in the right places until they formed this bottle around me — surrounding me on all sides. The glass is clear in places, not so clear where the glass is wavy. I can see some things just like they are. Other things become distorted with the waves, the irregularities of the glass.

The view is rather simple, very safe. There is comfort in not seeing too clearly, not seeing the sharp edges of hate and failure and betrayal. There is comfort in remaining protected and secure behind this facade of glass, away from the scene, yet in full view.

I feel safe here as I watch a blurry world walking around out there. I feel the relief of being separated from the competitive, stiff-armed rat race that catches up others and strangles them. I feel protected and calm, secure in my solitude.

I can manage the confinement of my glass walls, almost like a greenhouse that protects the plants inside. I cannot play hop scotch here, however. I can only remember what it was like, then—the smell of warm mud in spring, the giggles of little girls playing with the freedom of legs without snow pants.

I can't play any more; I can just watch — from inside this bottle.

Ring Around Rosie

Ring Around the Rosie, a pocket full of posies! Ashes, ashes, all fall down! Ring around Rosie, indeed. Her pockets full of posies. And she knew it. She danced. She pranced. She teased. She threw posies at them, every chance she got. Rosie loved it.

They came from afar to be treated to her posies. They wooed her — brought her gifts, breathed heavily on her, reached out for her... posies.

But Rosie wouldn't part with her posies. They were hers and she held onto them, her beloved posies. No one would share them with her. No one.

Until Rosie's wooers had had enough looking and reaching and heavy breathing. When they came to Rosie, many of them still breathing heavily, she smiled sweetly, flouncing her posies in front of them, cooing softly about how she loved her posies, teasing...

The wooers waited no longer. They came closer to her, reaching out toward her posies, but she squirmed away, twisting just out of their grasp. The wooers moved apart and began to circle Rosie, round and round until she no longer could wiggle away. Her smile became an edgy laugh as she tossed her curls and shook her posies. She would not share them... but there were too many, and they were all around her, grabbing at her from all directions. She turned, squirmed, tried to wriggle out between them, but there were too many. She dropped to her knees and attempted to crawl away, now whimpering, crying out for someone to protect her posies... but there were too many of them....

Ring around the Rosie,

A pocketful of posies.

Ashes, ashes, ashes...

THE THREE FACES OF ANGEL

Who is this woman known to those close to her as Angel?

I know her as having at least three faces because I've known her throughout her long life. There was that Angel with a dirty face, the child who hopped and skipped her way into the hearts of all who knew her. And there was the Angel who cleaned up dirty faces as the mother of six beautiful children. Now there is the Angel who spreads her love and caring with her neighbors, her family, and herself.

As the child Angel, she claimed she wore five invisible faces with the aid of *Inquy, Dinquy, Donquy, Jenry* and *Ring*! They were companions as she sought her place in the world — loyal friends and playmates to that little girl.

Angel was a girl who sat quietly, sometimes for seconds on end, watching her mother play the piano, then took over the keys and poked around until she found music in them. She watched her big sister practice tap-dancing lessons, carefully listening to the "seven-eight-nine shuffle-ball-change" until she could do it herself.

Angel didn't need the lessons, the learning of the rules and regulations of the arts. She simply watched and repeated what she saw. The stranger part is that she usually did it better, since she was learning-by-doing rather than taking instruction. That and the fact she possesses a natural energy to dance and sing and play music. Not all of us are blessed with those natural talents. Angel is.

As the mother Angel, she grew into womanhood alongside the love of her life. When Angel saw him, they both knew it was a lifelong affair. So they weren't surprised when their love produced six lovely children, three with her blue eyes and light colored hair and three with his brown eyes and dark hair.

Angel didn't need mothering lessons either. She came by it naturally, as she did with most of her life. She cuddled her children while instilling life's lessons into their beautiful heads. She sat up long nights with their fevers, eased the pains of their altercations, nudged them through their teenage trials, and watched without interference as they found their own life partners. Her greatest life challenge came when one of those darlings left this earth to try out a less troublesome place to experience the joys of eternity.

As the Angel of today, this extraordinary woman delights in sharing her talents with others who have lost the blessings that Angel holds onto. She causes the faces of others to light up as she tells her stories, or plays and sings the music that recalls earlier, younger times, younger loves. She draws and writes. Give her a subject and she'll draw you a picture or write a charming story to go with it. She composed a folio of stories that she shares with her grandchildren.

Today's Angel most notably has discovered her own strengths (yes, that's plural). Angel knows she can survive the tragedy of loss as much as she knows she has powers of creation within her. She accepts her ability to make a difference in the life of another. She accepts her talents developed in childhood to sing, write, draw, dance, and entertain others. And she accepts her strong capacity to look into the eyes of pain and withdraw the aches with her patience and love.

But most importantly, Angel has discovered ways to care for herself in all the important ways: physically, mentally, and spiritually. She holds onto intense beliefs in the goodness of others — and receives that goodness back from others. She recognizes the importance of knowing that the strengths she has showered on her children grow in a ratio to the love they return to her. Behind it all, she holds fast to a faith in her God, the greatest love of all.

Angel's three faces, in truth, are anchored by a heart that she wears on the outside where anybody can get at it. Angel continues to live a life of everlasting value through her caring, her knowing and understanding, and her undemanding and unending love.

I should know – I'm her sister.

Go Out And Play...

"Go out and play, Jamie." God, I hate holidays. I can still hear my mother telling me to go out and play, get out from underfoot. Then, I can hear my father telling me that idle hands make the devil's work, and god knows, I didn't want to do the devil's work.

Holidays were terror for me; they still are. Everybody's gone, out doing something, out playing, I guess. Nothing's open; school, stock market, post office, bank. Nobody's in their office — except me, of course. I'm here.

Where else would I be?

"Go out and play, Jamie. The sun is shining."

"I can't do that, Mom. Dad says that's the devil's work."

"Just go outside then. But get out of here."

Outside. What's there? Guess I could throw a ball at the garage door. But that doesn't get me anywhere. I just throw and catch, back and forth. Is that what the devil does?

Or I could walk, down along the river. Smell the freshness of the heavy spring rains that make the river rise. I can see where the rocks on the side got wet, way up there.

We had a big rain this spring, bigger than last year anyway. I wonder if that makes more fish or better fish, Dad? Dad and I liked to fish while we talked "business". Dad was always talking business with me. He said I'd take over his business some day so I had better be ready.

Dad said the only way to get ahead in this world is to work for yourself and work hard. He must have believed what he said because he was always working. He'd come home at the end of the day, open his briefcase, and go into his office downstairs. He was always on the telephone, even on weekends. Mom said he went to church Sundays because he could improve his business there.

Watch the birds and listen to their chatter as they flit from branch to branch. Are they playing? Or are they working? Is that their work to flit about and chirp? They could be gathering twigs and stuff for their nests. That would be work, wouldn't it? Then the mothers lay eggs, and that's got to be work. And raising the little babies so they can learn to fly. That's their job. Yeah, I'm sure that's their job. Raising the babies.

Too bad my parents didn't see that as work. Raising their kids. They didn't pay any attention to me at all unless I was doing homework or doing my chores. Scrub the back steps every Saturday, take out the trash every Thursday night, make my bed, clean my room. Hey, that was my work. What more did they want?

Stupid question. They wanted me to start my own business, sell the trash, open a home-chore business for the old ladies down the block, collect and sell old newspapers.

Here I am, in my own business now. Dad's retired and I'm the boss. I make the rules. I give everybody else a day off for a holiday, a day to play. Must be something in the genes that keeps me in when I'd rather be outdoors playing.

Question: or would I? Really?

Answer: If I enjoyed playing, I'd play, wouldn't I?

Maybe not. The devil's work, remember? Playing is bad. Mom wanted me to do it, maybe just to get me in trouble with Dad. They were always doing that to me. You know, playing me one against the other, *playing me*... interesting choice of words. They played me, played with me. I was some kind of toy they played with to compete with each other. Yes, that's rather clear now. I was their play, their entertainment. Everything else was work.

How do I feel being their toy? I feel used, sad... no, I feel unhappy... no, strong. No, I feel angry, yes, mad... damn mad. I feel furious. They used me! How dare they take a little kid and bat him back and forth like a badminton birdie. They used me to play their dirty little game of one-up.

"Go out and play, Jamie."

"Playing is the devil's work, Jamie."

And there's little Jamie in the middle. If I play, I'm condemned by Dad. If I don't play, I'm not pleasing Mother. Gotta figure this out.

There's only one thing to do. Disappear. Become invisible. Stay out of their way, both of them. Mom will think I'm playing; Dad will think I'm working.

Now, what becomes of their game?

HAROLD, HAROLD, MARVELOUS HAROLD

THE GREAT ROMANCE OF 1941

(Excerpt from *How We Fought World War II at William T. Sherman Elementary School*, the story of a little girl contending with life in grade school during a very long war.)

Harold Hoffman and Lili Deveroux spoke very little to each other. She watched him from a distance, followed him around the playground, stole peeks at him during class and managed to stand near him more often than he or anyone else noticed.

Harold was an outgoing boy who made friends easily; Lili was a shy girl who was drawn to his shining brown eyes. Their only contact in fourth grade was the seating arrangement that put them next to each other on the first day. During the first half of fifth grade, Harold was placed in another classroom, which was all right with Lili, since she had moved on to a gigantic crush on her fifth grade teacher, Mr. Kolmas. Still, the vision of Harold's sparkly dark brown eyes stayed with Lili.

Then came mid-year. Lili was moved to Miss Nicoud's room.

"Guess what, Megan…" Lili was panting as she caught up with her friend on the playground. The January day in 1941 had turned sunny and, while the air was still very cold, the sun's unexpected warmth boosted spirits.

"What?" Megan answered, barely missing a beat as she skipped rope. She had found a spot on the pavement that poked up clear between icy ruts. The feet of many children kept the snow and ice from piling up on the playground, and the friendly janitor occasionally took out a shovel to clear the play area. Today the sun was helping to melt off more of the ice.

"Guess who is sitting in the next row, two seats ahead of me!"

"You got Miss Nicoud, right?"

"Yes. You know that. I'm sorry you didn't get moved too. I just love Mr. Kolmas and think he's dreamy, even better looking than Clark Gable, but…"

"I'd say he's even better looking than John Payne. But now he's mine." Megan sang the last few words to the beat of the skip rope. "So, Lili, what's your big news?"

"Oh, almost forgot. No I didn't! Wait 'til you hear…"

"Well come on, Lil, spill! What's the news?" Megan stopped the rope and sidled up to her friend.

"Guess who's sitting in the …"

"I heard all that. I give up. Who is sitting in the next row, two seats up?" Megan was losing patience.

"Him. Harold Hoffman!" Lili waited for Megan to swoon. Like the girls did over John Payne.

But Megan only answered, "Lili, what's the use of mooning over Harold when you won't even speak to him? There he is, over by the fence. Go over and talk to him… now." Megan turned and pointed to the boys slapping each other on their backs to keep warm.

"Oh, I couldn't, Megan. I just couldn't."

"Why not? He won't bite."

"Yes he will… I mean… I know that… it's just…"

"Just nothing. Come on, I'll go with you." Megan tugged at Lili's hand, pulling off her mitten as she did.

Lili took the chance to hang back. "No, not now. I'll have to get up the nerve."

"And when will that be? When you've graduated from high school and he's gone off to college? Come on. Now!"

But Lili wouldn't budge. "I'd rather not, Megan, if you don't mind," she said very quietly. "Maybe tomorrow. I'll try to get up the nerve… tomorrow."

"All I can say is: what good is it being in class with Harold sitting across the aisle if you won't talk to him anyway? He might as well be in… in… Norway."

The practical odds were against a close friendship between Harold and Lili. Harold didn't play in the orchestra; Harold didn't sit on her side of the room once Miss Nicoud moved a few people around; Harold didn't like to draw. Harold liked to play baseball at recess; Harold liked to run and yell with his friends; and Harold disappeared in the opposite direction after school.

All she did know about this boy was that his brother was serving in the Army in Texas. In short, Harold and Lili seldom found each other in the same place, except back in fourth grade when both had become safety cadets. Even then, they shared the same duty corners only twice.

Lili suspected that Harold's family was German. "After all, Hoffman is a German name and the Germans took over France last summer," Lili's mother said. "Remember that your father's Deveroux family still has ties to France."

Still, Lili adored Harold and his gigantic deep brown eyes that sparkled — at least the idea of him. She confided to Megan that she thought he was the best looking boy in class, and the most popular. She sent him a valentine, making sure it was a comic one. Both Lili and Megan agreed that he probably was inaccessible to Lili. Still Lili adored him.

Harold became even more inaccessible after Laura Lanville moved in. Laura entered the lives of Miss Nicoud's fifth grade classroom a couple weeks after mid-term. As if the winter wasn't dragging on long enough and cold enough to make Lili miserable, here came interference in the form of a pretty fifth grade interloper.

Laura obviously came from a rich family since she wore store-bought dresses and had her hair curled every day "by a hairdresser," according to Megan and her rumor mill. "Nobody could have hair that curly naturally!" Megan had sided with her friend soon after Laura's arrival. "I'll bet she even puts face cream on at night, like her mother or her big sister!"

Laura sauntered into Miss Nicoud's class on a Monday morning and was assigned a seat directly in front of Harold. Lili immediately saw the writing on the wall as she watched him offer to help Laura with her books, her papers, her pencils, even her sweater; he held it out carefully and placed it around her shoulders, reminding Lili of how he had helped her on their first day of fourth grade.

Come on Harold, don't make such a jerk of yourself, she silently warned him from across the room.

At recess, Harold offered to show Laura the playground. He never showed the playground to Lili! At lunch, Harold and Laura walked home together in the opposite direction of Lili's home.

"Darn! I mean, drat!" she complained to Megan when they met that afternoon. "They even live near each other!"

"How's that for chutzpah?" Megan agreed. She loved using Yiddish words she had learned from her friend Minette. "Look at them mooning over each other! What a schnook!"

"She's got cheek all right," Lili agreed, not taking her eyes off her silent swain and his new conquest. Harold and Laura walked slowly toward the school building, looking at each other and nearly bumping into a fence. Harold was as smitten with Laura as Lili was smitten with Harold, an observance clear to just about everyone except Harold and Laura and Lili. But Lili didn't give up.

Before the story can continue, there are a few things necessary to know about how things were in Milwaukee in 1941.

Telephones were fairly new just before the war. City phones came with options that allowed users either unlimited service (at great expense) or limited service (two-outgoing-calls-a-day). Since Lili's family didn't use the phone much, her parents had chosen the limited service. They could make more than two calls, of course, but at a cost (five cents for each extra call). While that sounds infinitesimal looking backward, Lili's mother considered it substantial enough to discourage extra calls. After all, the Great Depression was still fresh in her memory. Telephone numbers then carried alpha names instead of prefixes. Families of both Lili and Harold were listed on the KI (Kilbourn) exchange. Phones also were on party lines, which meant each party was identified with a different ring. The code for Lili's family was three short rings. She didn't know the ring for Harold's family, but she'd soon find out.

Lili decided to telephone Harold, and she knew she had to plot carefully. Either she could wait for a day when she knew her mother hadn't used up the allotted two calls, or she could choose an opportunity when she was babysitting at the home of a family who had unlimited telephone service. She chose the latter.

Lili sat with Minette's little cousins on alternate Friday nights. Usually the parents attended temple services, and often they stayed out late with their friends. A couple weeks after Laura Lanville had come on the scene, Lili looked up Harold Hoffman's number in the phone book and memorized it so she would be ready on the next Friday when she would be babysitting late.

That night she made sure the children were tucked in and the house was quiet before she approached the phone. Lili sat down next to it about 8:30 and stared at the machine for a few minutes. She tried to imagine what she would say, how Harold would answer. How will I sound? What reason will I give for calling him? she wondered.

Homework... a work assignment... hadn't Miss Nicoud asked us to look up something? She couldn't remember. Probably not.

A whim? "I thought I'd just call up and chat." No, nobody just called up somebody to chat. Not in 1941. And certainly not Lili. She wasn't the chatting kind.

A question? Yes, a question that no one could answer except Harold Hoffman. Of course! "What is your address? I want to send you an invitation to..." But Lili had nothing to send out invitations for. Would Harold know?

Perhaps she ought to ask him about... but Harold and Lili had little in common — except her attraction to those deep brown eyes.

Lili continued to stare into space, wondering what reason she could give for calling on the telephone. She walked into the kitchen and drew a glass of water and sipped it slowly before returning to the telephone. She just wanted to talk to him, to hear his voice. She continued to stare at the telephone.

That's it! I'll call, wait for him to say Hello, then hang up. I don't have to speak. But would he find out it was me? He might. But unlikely if I just listen and hang up.

Lili dialed the number carefully. Somewhere in the night, along dark cables, a connection was made and the ringing began.

The phone rang the coded two short rings — once, twice, three times, again, and again. Lili's heart pounded. How long should she let it ring?

Then an interruption; someone picked up the telephone. Lili's heart stopped pounding; her heart stopped… period. Her breathing stopped. She heard a very sleepy "Hello" from a male voice, a fatherly voice. She gasped, gulped a mouthful of air and asked softly, "Is Harold home?"

"What?" asked the surprised voice. "Of course Harold is home. He's sleeping."

"Oh," Lili exhaled into the mouthpiece. "Oh," she repeated.

"Who is this?" the voice asked. "Do you know what time it is? Who is this?"

"I'm sorry," she whispered pathetically.

"It's almost midnight," the voice came back angrily.

"Oh," and she repeated, "oh," and hastily hung up the receiver. She glanced at the clock. Ten minutes before midnight. No wonder the voice was sleepy. She had let hours pass as she struggled to make her decision. Oh, I hope they don't know who I am. Oh me! How will I ever face Harold again?

But she did, and often. Now that she had made a contact with his private home life, he became a real living person to her instead of a fantasy. If he suspected the call was from Lili, he didn't show it, although his father questioned him for weeks. She learned that he lived just a couple blocks from her house. She would walk past the house (on the opposite side of the street), hoping to see him and afraid she might. She never caught so much as a glimpse of Harold... although she spotted his mother once.

Then Laura Lanville slipped out of their lives as abruptly as she had invaded them.

Over the next years, then into high school, Lili managed to approach Harold more comfortably, even starting conversations at times and listening to him answer questions she made up. They became almost-friends, somewhere between mere acquaintance and actual friendship. But, oh, those sparkly brown eyes haunted her for a very long time.

[Epilogue: Lili looked for Harold at their 40th high school class reunion. She had to look closely at nametags before she found him. The sparkle had left the brown eyes. Lili, a secure, successful attorney, approached her first love. "I'd know you anywhere," she lied. They chatted for a few moments (Lili had learned to chat), then Harold squinted at her nametag and asked casually, "And who did you say you are?"]

WATCH ME, DADDY

Watch me, Daddy. Watch me skip. I learned to skip today. I've tried so hard and watched my best friend skip. And she showed me how and now I can skip. Watch me, Daddy. Daddy... Daddy? Daddy?

You aren't watching me. You're going right past me to the nursery to watch my baby brother cry. Why won't you watch me? You used to watch me do everything, every little thing, but you don't watch me anymore.

Look, Daddy. I can ride my tricycle. See how well I can pedal with both my feet. And I can steer. It's just like you drive your car. Look, Daddy. Look at me on my tricycle. Look at me.

Daddy, you aren't looking at me. You're gazing off in the distance, looking at the sky, the trees, the birds, but not at me. Is something wrong, Daddy? Am I doing it wrong, Daddy? What's the matter, why aren't you looking at me?

See me, Daddy, see me roller skate. I wear the skate key around my neck and my skates stay on my feet. I like the cement especially, Daddy. Look how well I balance, and no, I don't fall down, much.

You aren't seeing me, Daddy. I think you're seeing something else. Is it my brother batting his ball over in the empty lot? Would you rather go see him play with his silly old ball?

Look at me, Daddy. See how I can ride my bicycle. I've practiced my riding all day, Daddy, why can't you see how hard I try, how daring I am to ride with one hand? See how I balance and go fast. See me, Daddy. See me ride my bicycle.

You're not watching me, Daddy. You're searching your briefcase for some papers, and listening to Mama crying in the kitchen, and you aren't watching me.

Did you know I learned to drive a car, just from watching you? Let me show you. I sit on the side of my bed and practice shifting gears. Let me do it for real… just for you, Daddy. Listen, Daddy. I've rehearsed this song just for you. I learned to play the piano so you'd be proud of me and now I've learned this song just for you. Listen, Daddy, I want you to hear this.

You're not listening, Daddy, you're talking to Mommy. You're talking about the house and you're not listening to me play. Oh, what must I do, Daddy, so you'll listen to me?

Look at this, Daddy. I'm able to turn a somersault backwards in the air and land on my feet. Look at this, Daddy, look at me. I learned gymnastics. I can do it. I try very hard to do difficult things so you'll see how good I am. Look at me turn a backward somersault, Daddy. Please look. Did you see my grades, Daddy? Do you see how I'm getting all A's? I studied hard to please you, so you'd be proud of me. Do you think I'm smart, Daddy?

You're not answering me. I think your head is still at work, still doing the office stuff. Oh, Daddy, I want you to know how hard I try to show you how well I learn gymnastics, how well I study and do things to please you. Why do you bring your work home in your head? You don't even talk to Mama anymore. Where are you, Daddy?

Notice how pretty I look, Daddy. Don't you see how pretty I look tonight, all dressed up for a special dance. I'm even wearing your favorite perfume. You said you liked it once and I bought some, just for you. Notice how nice I smell, how pretty I look.

Daddy, you don't notice when I'm dressed up. You don't notice me when I'm all fixed up for you. See how much I want to be pretty for you? Are you thinking about how Mother used to look? I'm not her, Daddy, I'm me. Notice me, Daddy. I'm going on a date.

Hey, Daddy-oh, look at your little girl, flying high, out with boys and flying high. Look at how naughty I've become, how grown up I am now. Look how your little girl can smoke cigarettes and drink beer and get high with the special stuff. Look at your little girl.

Can I get you to look at me now? You don't even want to notice when I do something wrong. Oh, Daddy, why can't you see how much I love you, how much I want you to know I'm alive, I'm here, right under your nose. I want to be a good girl for you, but you never seem to notice me when I'm good.

Daddy, give me your attention for a moment? Can you stop thinking about the office, my college bills, your mixed-up marriage and turn your attention to me. Here I am on this podium, giving a graduation speech that everyone else is listening to. And you're not here. Why couldn't you put off this business trip and be here for my college graduation? I'm giving a speech, for crying out loud. The most important moment of my life and you're not even in town.

Now hear what I'm saying, Daddy. I don't care if you want to leave Mom. I don't care if you can't stay with her anymore. I love you and I want you to love me. I want you to hear me when I scream at you. Are you deaf? Can't you hear that I need you? Oh, Daddy, why do you have to go away?

You've never heard me, or watched me. You've never seen what I can do, you've never noticed how pretty I am, you've never been there while I did something important. Why do I mean so little to you, your own flesh and blood, your own body mixed up in my genes? You were always too busy to watch me, and now you're going away. Don't you love me at all, not even a little bit?

Watch me, Daddy. Watch me swing my hips as I walk on these 4-inch heels. You've never seen me in anything as skimpy as this before. Watch me, Daddy. I can swing my hips and jiggle my body, and these guys will watch me. They sit with their drinks in their hand, and they don't even sip when I'm on stage. They don't look at anything else in the room, just me. See how they watch me move, Daddy? Look how they want me to take my clothes all off. Do you see how I move when I know they're watching me? Do you see how pretty I look with the spotlight on my bare skin? Can you see how they appreciate what I'm doing? *They* notice me. *They* are paying attention. Why not you, Daddy? Why won't *you* watch me, Daddy? Oh, Daddy, please. Look at me!

SECTION IV

PLAYS

ZAP!

A ONE-ACT PLAY

CAST:

GOD — Woman wearing white flowing robes, what else? With strong sense of herself.

VOICE — God's Mother. Offstage only.

AHDAM — Young virile man, the type to be the first man on earth!

EVE-ening — Young strong woman, the type to be the first woman on earth!

ETHEL — Earth mother type, 39, maybe a bit older.

FRED — Ethel's husband, 40-ish, friendly neighbor.

MOSES — Little old lady with a stone tablet.

SCENE: A garden that fills most of the stage, a few trees and plants and a hide-behind shrub to hide the nakedness of the players. At Stage Right are porch steps to sit on. (This side remains dark until needed.)

[As the curtain goes up, the stage is dark.]

VOICE:

What on earth are you doing?

GOD

Earth! That's what I'm doing, making my new planet — out of earth.

VOICE

What's that squishing sound?

GOD

I'm working on my first human creation. Having a bit of trouble. Can't see what I'm doing. And the clay is hard to handle.

VOICE

For Heaven's sake, you're God. Why don't you create light?

GOD

Wish I'd thought of that. Okay, here goes — Let there be light. Zap!

[At the sound of Zap, thunder rolls and the lights go on.]

VOICE

That's better.

[As the lights go on, a man (AHDAM) in a three-piece suit stands next to God. squints at the light, then skitters into the shadows.]

VOICE

What was that?

GOD

My first human creation.

VOICE

In a three-piece suit? What were you thinking? Can't you get anything right?

GOD

You're right, Mom. What was I thinking? Let it evolve. I'll zap this first model. Zap!

[As GOD says "zap", thunder rolls and AHDAM disappears.]

VOICE

Want to try again?

GOD

Okay, but this time I do it my way. With the lights on, I can create a human in my image. Watch this, Mom. Zap!

> [At the Zap, thunder rolls and
> EVE appears (behind the bush).
> Long hair covers her intricate parts
> and she's smiling.]

GOD

Ah, this is a good thing.

VOICE

About time, Miss Almighty Goddess. What do you call it?

GOD

She looks like Woman to me.

VOICE

If you insist. What do you do next?

GOD

There is much to be done. Creating a world isn't easy. But stand back and let me go to work. Let's see. We've got light and dark. Next I'll create water and land. Zap!

> [At each sound of Zap, thunder rolls.]

GOD

And I'll create sunshine and call it California, and rain and call it Seattle. Zap! Zap!   [Thunder]

GOD

Next I'll populate the land. Great cedars, Zap. Mighty oaks, Zap. Graceful willows, Zap. Begonias, Zap.

VOICE

Enough with the zap already. Hold the thunder until she's finished!

> [Thunder tool falls to floor offstage
> with clattering sound.]

GOD

Where was I? Begonias...(pause but no thunder)

...orchids, sunflowers, deer and terrier,

Wildebeests and snakes...mustn't get scarier!

Carrots, rutabagas and azalea,

Violets, beans and arendalia.

Apples, celery, walnuts, could

Make Waldorf salad, and that is good!

VOICE

Ouch!

GOD

What? You're expecting me to be a poet too?

Gnats and bats and even rats,

Cougars and huskies, and alley cats,

Caribous and even gnus,

Cockatoos and manitous...

VOICE

Wait a minute! Isn't that manitees?

GOD

Whatever... Cows and squirrels and elephants.

Mosquitoes and thistles, for bits of balance.

Gazelles and butterflies, what a wonder!

Zap, zap, zap. (looking up) Now you can thunder.

[Sound of thunder]

GOD

Thank you. But there's more. There are still the streams and
great oceans to fill. Let's see. Salmon, a must, shark and
cod, Ah I love being God.
Then I'll add seals and whales and deep-sea goo.
Maybe haddock, eel, and walrus too.
Can't overlook trout in the brook…
And catfish, marlins and tuna to hook.
And sharks and dolphins, seahorse and minnow,
Seaweed and kelp…

VOICE

Kelp? Help!

GOD

Quiet! I'm on a roll. Kelp and lobster and shrimp and mahi
mahi.   [Thunder]

GOD

Wait, I didn't say Zap…   [Thunder]

GOD

Cute! Well, you get the idea. I can always add more later.
Right now I want to get back to the woman in the garden.
Perhaps it's time to create a second creature as a
companion piece, now that I can see what I'm doing. Okay,
give me a zap!

[Thunder and AHDAM appears

next to EVE, behind the bush, unclad]

VOICE

What is that?

GOD

I think I'll call it Man, a shortened version of Woman.

VOICE

Psst! They're uncovered. You didn't finish. No fur or wool or scales. Did you notice?

GOD

Hold your horses. I haven't created Chanel yet. I'm doing the best I can. First I have to name them. I'll call the woman Eve, as in EVE-ning, when she glows, and as in EVE-olve, which she'll do.

VOICE

What about him?

GOD

Let's have some fun. I'll go into the garden and I'll name him after the first thing I see. I'll call it out and that will be his name. Here goes.

[God starts into the garden and...]

VOICE

Watch out for the alligator...

[Trips over the alligator]

GOD

Ah! Damn!

VOICE

Ahdam? That's it? That's what you'll call him?

GOD

I didn't mean…

VOICE

You never do. Oh well, he could do worse. He could be called Myrtle or Rosemary.

GOD (to Ahdam)

Hey, honey, come over here.

AHDAM

(Shakes his head) No way. I'm not dressed.

GOD

That's what I want to talk to you about. Come here!

AHDAM

Who do you think you are anyway? God?

GOD

Who do you think I am? Whoopi Goldberg?

[AHDAM Approaches the edge of the bush.]

GOD

That's far enough. I'm giving you and Eve some cotton stuff, and you can find some sheep and clip the wool. Then you can make yourselves some clothes. I'll even toss in a spinning wheel… and a loom… Zap (thunder).

[GOD motions to EVE to go with AHDAM.]

GOD

Meanwhile, I'll be off to see what I can do about the deserts and the mountains. Difficult places to populate. Be back in a few days.

[Blackout. When the lights come up again,
AHDAM and EVE are clothed in muu-muus or togas.
EVE lounges in the sun, fashioning a wreath of hollyhocks
for her hair. GOD enters]

GOD

I have had such a time these last few days. Would you believe I had to do the camel twice?

EVE

Do you like our clothes? Ahdam wouldn't let me use more than a few dyes, but I managed to whip up this little number.

AHDAM

She wants to make everything bright and cheery. Me? I like gray. So, what's kept you so busy? It's been days.

GOD

I've been having a great time, making up exotic things to grow around the earth, making critters that hop and fly and wiggle and swim, and tossing things like turtles and frogs into ponds. But I'm tired. I've been at this creating business for six days. I'll have to think of more things later. For the moment, I need to rest, to meditate... even though I know this is a good thing.   (GOD turns to EVE as she speaks.]

EVE

(Yawns) Yes, meditate.

GOD

Don't you have anything to do?

EVE

No. Ahdam won't let me work. He says women are too fragile to work, so here I sit. And I'm bored.

GOD

(To Ahdam) I'll give the orders around here. (To Eve) Eve, you have the same free will that Ahdam has. It's up to you to choose what you want to do.

EVE

Well then, I choose to record the beauty around me. I choose to create pretty things to decorate my tree house. I choose to organize a team of...

AHDAM

Wait a minute. There isn't anyone around to form a team. I have work to do. See you later.   [AHDAM leaves]

EVE

I didn't think of that. Sorry, God, I don't wish to complain, but I think I need more people.

GOD

I get it. You want more creatures around who are like you.

EVE

Well, yes...

GOD

Somebody to talk to, whisper secrets to, yell at... fix your hair with, do your nails, exchange recipes...

EVE

What are recipes?

GOD

You'll find out soon enough. I think you'd like what I will call a friend...

EVE

Sort of. That's pretty much what I've been thinking about.

GOD

Then that man of yours isn't enough.

EVE

He's always busy. He's always off doing his own stuff and he doesn't talk to me about what he's doing. As a matter of fact, he pretty much leaves me alone.

GOD

Where did he go just now? What's he doing?

EVE

I guess he's up in the apple orchard again. He's probably picking the new crop for his concoction.

GOD

Concoction?

EVE

He made a batch with the last apples he harvested. Pulled those pretty red baubles off the branches, ground them up and let them sit for a few weeks until they got all frothy. Then he drained off the juice and drank it. Made him wobbly and woozy for a while. He said terrible things to me and even took a swipe at me. I've never seen Ahdam nasty like that before.

GOD

Ah Damn!

AHDAM

(Just coming through the trees) Yesh?

[AHDAM wobbles over to EVE and GOD

and sees they are angry.]

GOD

I wasn't calling you. But now that you're here, you might tell me just what you're doing up in the apple orchard.

AHDAM

Well, I…

GOD

Did I give you permission to pick the apples? I don't think so. And I certainly didn't give you permission to make moonshine out of them.

AHDAM

Moonshine? Ish that what you call it? Pretty good schtuff.

GOD

You've blown it, mister. Here I set you up in this beautiful garden, give you food to eat, water and lattes to drink, another human like you to be a companion, and you go off and screw it up. Oh Ahdam. You just don't get it, do you?
                              [God moves off and circles the two.
                                      She thinks out loud.]

GOD

Perhaps Eve is right. Perhaps there ought to be more human creatures. Oh, but then Ahdam would have someone to help him make more moonshine. They'd probably start harvesting the grass to eat or *God* forbid… oh, that's me… I forbid, smoke. Or they'd get together and throw big parties to drink the moonshine.
                              [God shakes her head and
                                moves in the other direction]

GOD

On the other hand, more people might put a damper on Ahdam's busy work. They might be a good influence on him. And Eve definitely needs to have more people around. If Ahdam isn't going to keep her company, perhaps she ought to have other friends.

> [GOD moves back to AHDAM and EVE, who is trying to sweep AHDAM's unruly hair out of his eyes. AHDAM stares blindly off into the distance.]

GOD

Okay, here's what I've decided. Here's what we'll do. The two of you will have to leave the garden.

AHDAM

EVE-icted?

GOD

No, Ahdam-victed... (pause)... my little joke. Anyway, out you go. I'll create other people for you to mix with. But you'll have to behave, keep yourselves covered when they're around. They won't be... well... family exactly, so find yourselves some more fig leaves and wool and, Ahdam, go make a closet to hold your new clothes.

AHDAM

Whatsh a closet?

GOD

You'll figure it out.

> [AHDAM and EVE begin to gather up their things to leave the garden.]

GOD

One other thing. I'll zap you a few friends, but you'll have to help me with this people-producing thing. Let's see if you can figure out a way to create your own humans.

EVE

But we're not God. How can we do this?

AHDAM

Eve, she's given us a challenge. We can play God.

GOD

(Scowling) Just be careful what you play at.

[Lights out. When they come up,
GOD surveys the work of EVE and AHDAM.
Now the steps of the house are visible.
Bowls and baskets strewn around.]

GOD

Will you look at that?

VOICE

They did *that* themselves? No zaps?

[EVE and AHDAM enter carrying a bushel basket of
something, looking very domestic.]

GOD

Seems as if. They've planted a vegetable garden, gathered
some cows and chickens and built pens for them. They've
got a fairly self-sufficient little ranch here.

EVE

Who are you talking to?

GOD

My mother.

EVE

Your mother?

AHDAM

Mother of God!

GOD

Of course. Everybody has a mother. Even God. Not everyone has a father, if you catch my drift.

VOICE

Careful with the innuendo there. Any new people around yet?

GOD

You'll see. I've been zapping up a few in my spare time. Here come their neighbors now.

[FRED and ETHEL come around the corner and greet EVE and AHDAM]

AHDAM

Hello. I'm Ahdam and this is my woman Eve.

ETHEL

And this is Fred and I am Ethel.

EVE

Are you the new neighbors God promised us?

FRED

Well, I'm not a neighbor, but I play one on TV.

ETHEL

(Elbows him) Oh, Fred.

EVE

What do we do now? Want to play a game? Dance? Or something?

FRED

Why not? (Puts his arm around AHDAM's shoulders) You say your name is Ahdam. What do you do for a living?

AHDAM

I'm not quite sure. I think it's called farming. Maybe it's what *you* just called it… living. Want to come see my orchard?

[FRED and AHDAM move offstage to the orchard]

EVE

They have a surprise waiting for them. God has removed all the apples from the orchard. Replaced them with oranges. They'll have to find something else to do.

ETHEL

When they get back, let's teach them to dance.

EVE

Good idea. In the meantime, want to see my house?

GOD

(Entering) Now that's the way things are supposed to be — men toiling in the fields, women caring for the house.

VOICE

What? Haven't I taught you better?

GOD

We'll see how they work that one out over the next few thousand years. Have you noticed how Ahdam is looking at Eve lately? I'm wondering if he hasn't come up with some way to help me with the People First program.

VOICE

Oh, that's what you call it now?

GOD

I saw them out in the barn yesterday and Ahdam wasn't thinking about the horses. I'm sure he's noticed just how strong and agile and soft and warm she can be.

VOICE

And she's got a gleam in *her* eye too. I notice those things.

GOD

You would.

VOICE

Beg your pardon?

GOD

You're pardoned.

VOICE

Here they come. I've got to see how they get these guys to dance.

[EVE and ETHEL come out of the house as AHDAM and FRED return from the orchard.]

AHDAM

Would you believe there isn't a single apple in the orchard.

FRED

Just a bunch of orange looking things. Wonder what they're called.

EVE

Ethel and I are going to teach you two to dance.

AHDAM

What's dance?

ETHEL

It's where two people hold onto each other and move their feet to music.

FRED

What's music?

EVE

You hum. Like this…

[EVE hums , takes AHDAM's hands and they start to dance. ETHEL does the same with FRED.
Music offstage.
AHDAM noticeably comes closer to EVE.]

AHDAM

I like this dance thing. Good game.

EVE

Be quiet and don't step on my toes.

[The dancing continues for a moment.]

FRED

Er, neighbors, I think Ethel and I'll be on our way. We just thought of something to do over at our place. See you soon.

ETHEL

Goodnight. And thanks for the nice party.

AHDAM

Uh-huh (he's engrossed with EVE).

EVE

Yeah, see you (she's engrossed with AHDAM) Ah, Ahdam, could you rub my shoulders, just a bit. (They stop dancing and he rubs her shoulders) Lower. Lower.

[Lights fade and go dark.
When lights come up,
EVE has grown a noticeable belly.
She and AHDAM sit on the steps shelling peas]

EVE

Ahdam, I've been feeling a bit queasy lately. Do you think it's something I've eaten?

AHDAM

You don't eat that much. I've noticed you barely touch the greens I bring you.

EVE

You know what would taste good? Shrimp. Yes, shrimp from the sea. Can you find me some?

AHDAM

I'll try.

[AHDAM moves off. EVE calls after him…]

EVE

Oh, and if you find some avocados or lemons, would you bring them home too?   [GOD enters]

GOD

Nature has taken its course. I knew they could do it. Look at her

VOICE

She'll be big as a house. Not too long.

EVE

God, is that you?

GOD

Yes, my child.

EVE

God, what is happening to me? Tell me what's going on.

GOD

Oh Eve, sweetie. You are creating a human, just like I asked.

EVE

Naw! No, I've watched you. I've seen you go zap and there's another person in front of you. You never did it *this* way?

GOD

Wait just a little while longer and you'll see. When you feel the moment is near, find a quiet place, maybe out in the stable where the new hay smells sweet and no one will bother you. Lie down on the hay and wait. I promise you a miracle. You'll see.

EVE

If I didn't know you could do it, I'd...

GOD

Trust me. I promise a miracle.

[GOD moves away from the steps.]

GOD

I've been thinking.

VOICE

Again?

GOD

I think it's time to add some ground rules here. Our young friends have several neighbors now and they're about to start a family...

VOICE

That's what you're calling it?

GOD

That's what it is! A family. I have spoken.

VOICE

(Laughing) Got it, God!

GOD

As I started to say… we need to add some ground rules, and soon. I think I'll send for my friend Moses. That's the creature I concocted last week as a prototype old person. Zap!   [Thunder]

GOD

Not now! I (whispering) zapped and just like that there's this old creature — wise and strong, a born leader, you might say.

VOICE

Born… leader… you're good. So, are you sending for this Moses?

GOD

I have spoken!

VOICE

Again with the spoken?

GOD

Don't interrupt. I'm calling in Moses — to set down some guidelines for life, something to help these creatures… the humans anyway… live better lives.

VOICE

I can't wait.

[God moves to background.
AHDAM returns with carry-out shrimp,
and avocados and lemons.
Joins EVE on the steps.]

AHDAM

Brought you everything you wanted. Shrimp, avocado, lemons…

EVE

That was fast. Can you dig up some sweet potatoes to go with the shrimp?

AHDAM

(Grumbling) I hope that whatever has gotten into you… (beat)… goes away soon. You're wearing me out with all these chores.

EVE

God says we're creating a human.

AHDAM

Can't be. She just zaps and there's one here. Why go through all this…?

EVE

God says that it will be a miracle.

AHDAM

This I've got to see. Do I have to be there to make it happen?

EVE

Apparently not. God said for me to go to the barn alone when it's time.

AHDAM

Doesn't sound like I have anything to do with this creation business.

EVE

Just keep me company. What would you rather be doing? Hanging out with the neighbors? Playing one of their new games. I've heard they have one now where they line up sticks and roll a melon to make them fall down.

AHDAM

Yes, I played yesterday. Kept rolling the melon into the ditch.

EVE

Isn't it called a gutter?

AHDAM

Whatever. I'm better at the other games, the ones where a bunch of guys hammer at each other until the other falls down.

EVE

(Patting her belly) Won't be long now and maybe you'll have other things to occupy your time.

AHDAM

(Looking offstage) Eve, somebody's coming.

EVE

Is it Ethel? She said she might come by today.

AHDAM

No, looks like an older woman. A very wrinkly woman. And she's carrying something. Looks like a big stone… or a canvas.

[MOSES enters.]

MOSES

(Approaches) Good day. Have I got the right place? Is this the ranch of Eve and Ahdam?

AHDAM

You've found us. Who are you? And what do you want?

MOSES

My name is Moses. But most folks just call me Grandma. God sent me to lay out some ground rules for living. Got 'em right here. All spelled out and numbered.

EVE

You didn't have to, really.

MOSES

Oh yes I did. When God speaks...

AHDAM

Here, let me take them and stand them against the house.

MOSES

(Sitting down slowly) That was a long trek. Been on the road for forty days and forty nights, even had to take a hike up Mount Sinai for a spell. Had lots of adventures.

EVE

Maybe you should write a book.

MOSES

Just might do that. Now that I've written these Commandments...

AHDAM

Commandments?

MOSES

Yes, that's what She wants to call the ground rules.
Commandments.

EVE

What were some of your other adventures?

MOSES

Well, girl, I had to get across the Red Sea. Would you
believe… no, you wouldn't. But I made it. Then I passed a
burning bush. That's when I got this message from God.
She sure knows how to get your attention.

EVE (Patting her tummy)

She sure does.

MOSES

Why are you so big, if you don't mind my asking?

EVE

I'm creating a human. God says it's a miracle. And it's in
there, kicking and kicking like crazy. Probably wants to get
out.

MOSES

I've heard about her miracle and you're right. If it's kicking
like that, you might want to grab a blanket and head for the
barn.

EVE

And I might just be doing that… (groan)… soon.

MOSES

Yes, I think it's time.   [Helps EVE stand up.
                                She reaches for a blanket
                                and walks slowly offstage.]

AHDAM

Do you want me to go with you?

EVE (calling back)

No. I need some time to myself. I'll call if I need you. If I'm not back in a couple hours, come find me.

MOSES

It'll be all right, son. She's just the first in a long line of women who'll be going through this. And she pretty much has to do it alone.

AHDAM

But won't I be… a… father? Isn't that what God called it?

MOSES

You've done your bit.

AHDAM

Have I?

MOSES

Remember the night you two danced… yes, I know all about it. You might practice some new words: Respect and Trust and Love. (Points to the Commandments) That's what these things are all about.

[Sound of baby crying in the barn. AHDAM gets up, takes MOSES' arm, and they walk toward the sound.]

GOD

What he'll see when he gets there is a very tired Eve lying back in the hay, cradling her new-born miracle in her arms as the tiny head bobs about seeking nourishment.

VOICE

What that man will feel is what for centuries a man will feel when he realizes he's part of a family now.

GOD

You got that right, Mom. This is a very good thing. I think I'll let them create all their own people from here on.

EVE

(Voice from the barn) Thank you, God.

AHDAM

Yes, thank you, God. You're right. This is a miracle.

VOICE

Zap!   [Thunder]

GOD

Thanks, Mom!

[Curtain]

WORKING OUT

A ONE-ACT PLAY

CAST OF CHARACTERS (2)

HE: A 53-year-old man, slightly paunchy, maybe balding, with a laid-back disposition. He's recently been laid off and is trying to establish a business as freelance photographer, a lifelong hobby that he hopes to turn into income. He wears rag-tag sweat pants and T-shirt, and sounds edgy, frustrated, worried.

SHE: A 50-ish woman, in fairly good shape, with graying hair and a caring manner. She has been a housewife and mother all her life, but is facing the empty nest, since her sons recently have left home. She wears a coordinated sweatsuit. Her bossiness covers a lonely and restless spirit.

SCENE

A gym — two exercise bicycle machines face the audience. During the Workout, HE and SHE pedal as they talk, with deviations as indicated. As the lights go up, HE is struggling with the controls at the machine as SHE does some stretches nearby. Her bones crack as she bends over.

HE: Judas Priest! Was that you?

SHE: Sorry?

HE: Were those your bones cracking? You okay?

SHE: Of course. Things always crack when you get to be...
a certain age.

HE: (Fumbling with the controls.) Damned technical stuff!

SHE: Need some help?

HE: Guess so. I got it started, but what's all this for?

SHE: Punch that button there and select the workout you
want.

HE: Huh?

SHE: You know, easy, moderate... you a first timer?

HE: Yeah, my wife says I should work out.

SHE: Smart lady. Here, try the Easy. You can work up.

HE: Thanks. You sound like a pro. Come here often?

SHE: Sorta. Couple times a week.

HE: That's often?

SHE: For me it is. You?

HE: My first time, or could you tell. Got a job?

SHE: Had one, lost it.

HE: Me too. (pause) Too bad. Where'd you work?

SHE: Home. I have children... I mean, we had children, my
husband and I... but they left.

HE: Empty nest something?

SHE: Sorta. The nest once had children and a missing
father. Now the father is back home, laid off, and the
children are missing. Ironic, huh!

HE: Yeah. Same with me... you know, the missing father.
Until I retired. Now my wife says I'm underfoot.

SHE: There, start pedaling at a comfortable speed.

[HE starts to pedal.]

HE: Like this?

SHE: Now go a notch faster and try to keep it there.

HE: And I thought you never forgot how to ride a bicycle. Didn't have all these gadgets when I was a kid!

SHE: Lots of things have changed since then. [They pedal in silence for a bit.] What were you interested in as a kid?

HE: Can't remember. Playing baseball, riding bicycles, and pictures, I guess.

SHE: Thought you couldn't remember.

HE: Well I do know I was interested in pictures.

SHE: In magazines? Or as in… taking pictures? With a camera?

HE: Yeah. I loved it. I'm kinda considering doing it now — for a kinda business. But my wife says it's a waste of time.

SHE: Sounds like a long lost dream, huh?

HE: Yeah!… What's this button?

SHE: Use that to control the resistance. The difference between an easy ride and a harder one.

HE: Got it! No resistance, easy ride, no results! Take the hard road, you risk more, but you get more out of it.

SHE: Interesting theory. (Pause.) Sometimes you strain too hard and pull something. (Points) Look at that… that old guy… comes here all the time and just keeps plugging…. Talk about doing it the hard way, he must have arthritis or something… but he hangs in… staying healthy… maybe for his family.

HE: Looks tired to me. That's why I'm here. To get healthy…

SHE: Or because… your wife says …

[They chug on in silence for a moment.]

SHE: I like cycling here where I can watch the walkers around the gym. (Points) Oh-oh, here come the kiddies.

HE: They got kids here?

SHE: School kids… while their parents work out. Look at that little guy… chin pushed out, setting the pace… reminds me of…

HE: You got kids? Of course you do. Reminds you of your…?

SHE: My son, yes. Determined chin, won't slow up, just keeps on going.

HE: Maybe he wants to come in first… you think?

SHE: (Muses)… Probably. That's my oldest. He's a musician like his grandpa, determined to show his mom he can make it… plays saxophone.

HE: He's good, huh! Sometimes you gotta find what makes you happy and do it. The kid… that one there (points)… and your sax player… they're doing it.

SHE: Okay, wise guy. (Points) What about that little girl… see? The one out of step. Can't decide which leg is ahead, out of breath, but she keeps going. (SHE waves a thumbs-up to her.)

HE: She'll make it. She's not a natural, like the other kid, but she's trying. Like I said, you gotta follow your dream. Look, she's puffing faster. You encouraged her. I can see how you enjoy this people watching.

SHE: Maybe. When you're puffing that hard, tho, it takes more than a thumbs-up to keep you going.

HE: Sometimes the puffing is what keeps you alive.

[Silence for a while. HE begins to strain.]

SHE: Hey, take it easy. You're not riding in the Grand Prix!

HE: Maybe I will some day.

SHE: Dreamer![More silence.]

HE: You don't dream?

SHE: No... well, maybe. I used to. It's been so long I can't remember.

HE: I'll bet you did. Ever wanna be a dancer? or a movie star? or an artist? or...

SHE: Oh yeah... a long time ago. I wanted to be a lounge singer, you know, the kind that drapes herself over the piano wearing a slinky black gown and belts out the blues. Wow, that's an old dream. Haven't thought of that in years.

HE: You'd be good.

SHE: What do you mean?

HE: Draped over the piano... wearing a slinky... you know... (HE winks.)

SHE: It's been a long time since I've... dreamed. Guess that's what being a wife and mother does to you.

HE: Sorry.

SHE: No need to be sorry. It's what I chose. And I've enjoyed every moment... well, almost every moment... not the diapers.

HE: But now? The blues coming back? The kids gone?

SHE: (Pause.) Probably that's it. The boys are gone... and... hey, I like that: "the blues are coming back."

HE: (Points) There... do you see that old woman? Do you think she ever wanted to sing the blues?

SHE: Nah, she's a trouble-maker that one. She's shuffling, not really working out, just walking, as if someone told her she had to. They do that, you know, bring people here to work out — from the nursing homes and home school families. There, like those teenagers... plodding along as if they'd rather be strung up and beaten than take another step.

HE: (Points) How about those young girls jogging rather jauntily... get that? Jogging? Jaunty?

SHE: Cute. You a poet or something?

HE: Naw, I just take pictures.

SHE: That's what you said... you're in the photography business.

HE: Don't I wish! Naw, I'm just thinking about it. Setting up a business is a lot harder than I thought. I figured retirement was the best time to start doing something I really enjoy — and I enjoy taking pictures. But making a business of it... that's another...

SHE: Your wife doesn't think you'll make it?

HE: You got it! She keeps telling me to get a real job. Worked a lifetime at Boeing — at least it felt like a lifetime. Now they set me free, with a little booty, and I want to ...

SHE: Surely you have... obligations.

HE: Oh yeah! Big time responsibilities: the house, the wife, a kid in college. But when I start making money on the photography, we'll be in pretty good shape.

SHE: If... if you start making money. Sounds a bit risky to me.

HE: Sometimes you have to risk to get anywhere.

SHE: Tell me about risk! My dad's a musician. Like my son. Out on their own — they don't have... what I guess you'd call "responsibilities". My dad was a hippy. Still is. Left my mom when we were teenagers. (Pause. Points) That old woman is back around, still shuffling. She looks like... oh god, she looks like my mother.

HE: Don't they call that the Sandwich Generation — taking care of both kids *and* parents.

SHE: It fits. My freeloading musician dad drops in when he's hungry or... near. (SHE searches his face.) Like now. He called yesterday and said he was... near.

HE: Oh. (pause) You weren't expecting him?

SHE: Oh no. He just pops in. But again, he may not.

HE: I always wanted to run away and join the hippies. But I think you have to sing to get in and... I don't sing.

SHE: Not a bit? A teeny bit? The national anthem?

HE: I'll bet your mother sings.

SHE: Why would you say that?

HE: Your dad's a musician. I'll bet they made beautiful music together once. Your mother still... plugging along?

SHE: She's living in California, at least for now.

HE: (Points) That one looks like she belongs in a nursing home. She has that faraway look, like she doesn't even know where she is.

SHE: Mom gets like that sometimes. They think it could be the onset of Alzheimer's, but they aren't sure. She got lost once, and she loses things.

HE: Don't we all. Maybe I'm getting to that place too.

SHE: Oh no, you're doing fine. Look at that — you're burning calories. How many...? Look... you've gone four-tenths of a mile so far.

HE: (Grumpy) Lucky me. Cripes! I'm going nowhere, fast. Like that old duffer — just plugging along.

SHE: Having fun yet?

HE: Wish I had a donut.

SHE: Your wife was smart to send you here. You think she's bossy, huh?

HE: Nah, she's not so bossy… I guess she's just looking out for me. I wish my mother had looked out for my father. He died too young. Maybe I oughta listen to what they say about it running in the family.

SHE: Your dad was how old?

HE: Fifty-four.

SHE: And you? Let me guess… fifty-four.

HE: Yeah! Next year. If I live.

SHE: (Triumphantly) And you will live if you keep this up. You're doing just fine. Aren't you glad you came? Keep it up. Rome wasn't built in a …

HE: Yeah…? Wasn't my decision… my wife's.

SHE: But you took her advice.

HE: Wish she'd take mine.

SHE: Your advice?

HE: Yeah.

SHE: And that is…

HE: I wish she'd… uh, "become a lounge singer"… you know (grins at HER), like you. Do something for *herself*. I've saddled her with so much over the years — raising my sons, my mother with her long list of gripes every time she visits, and now there's the boy at college — she misses him…

SHE: Real empty nest syndrome.

HE: Oh yeah. (Points) Hey, look at that little girl. She's really racing around the track now. Looks like your thumbs-up did something for her.

SHE: Wish I could thumbs-up myself. I'm not sure what I want. With my boys out of the house and my husband pre-occupied…

HE: Pre-occupied?

SHE: Well, he has *his* work and *his* dreams.

HE: Maybe then it's your turn to follow some dreams. Come on, now, tell me what you'd really like to do.

SHE: Watch your controls there. When that light blinks, you're supposed to grab the handles and let it take your heart rate.

HE: Like this?

SHE: Yes. Good. See? You're up to 110. How high did you program?

HE: Huh?

SHE: Never mind, it'll tell you when your heart breaks… I mean…

HE: That's a good one. A machine to tell you when your heart breaks.

[Silence]

HE: Your mom. Have you ever invited her to live with you? Might fill up some of the nest.

SHE: Oh no! No! No! She's perfectly happy living near my sister in California. I'm not very good with old people, and my sister is. I've been pretty worried about putting her in a nursing home. She probably could use it; but I hate to think of her leaving her own house. (Pause) Still, the last time she visited, she nearly set the house on fire when I let her help in the kitchen.

HE: Oh?

SHE: I didn't notice when she left a towel in the oven. It smoked a bit... could have been worse... but I worry that it could happen while she's alone.

HE: Sounds like your sis might find a place for her there. You can always visit her. And if she visits you, just keep a close eye on her. Mothers are flexible. (HE grins at her.)

SHE: Sounds wise. I didn't realize you were so wise.

HE: Oh yeah, they call me a wise guy at home.

SHE: I'll just bet. Your mother doesn't have that problem, huh? She just...

HE: ...visits and gripes. She almost remarried a couple years ago, but I guess her intended got a taste of her disposition. Anyway, it's good she's still alive.

SHE: Do you suppose she misses your father more than she's telling you? That can make a woman very cranky.

HE: I know she isn't pleasant to have around, but she does like to visit me and my wife — she says it reminds her of her own family... back when...

SHE: So, Mr. Wise Guy, you handle your mother. What would *you* suggest I do about my father, the freeloading guitar player.

HE: When he comes to visit, drape yourself over the piano and sing with him.

SHE: (Laughs) Oh that would be great! (Pause.) You know, might not be such a bad idea. At least he doesn't need a nursing home... yet. Maybe I can get my son to drop by... and they can jam together.

HE: The son that looks like that one (points)?

SHE: That determined little bugger! Look how he just keeps going, like that rabbit. He's so cute. He does remind me of my boy. You said you had a son in college?

HE: He's just left. My wife hates it that he's chosen a school across the country, but he wanted to be on his own. He's the youngest, the last to go, and she feels real lost without him.

SHE: Does that bother you?

HE: Not until now. I guess I didn't realize how lost she can be — her being a professional mother and all. Now she's lost her job... like you... and maybe I never asked about her dreams. Just assumed that being a mother was a lifetime job and she didn't dream.

SHE: Oh she dreams... a lot... but she probably doesn't expect them to come true. Dreams are like that. They're quick — in and out and lost. Something like yours, I would imagine.

[Silence]

HE: For so many years I pushed those crappy pencils at Boeing, waiting for the day I could retire and start my own photo business — take pictures all day and develop and print them all night. The ironic part is that now that Boeing's set me free, the photography business has taken a complete new turn. Everything's on computers these days.

SHE: And you don't enjoy that as much? Have you tried it?

HE: You seem pretty computer savvy. Don't you think it would be different?

SHE: Not much more different than... say... composing music on the computer. They do that, don't they?

HE: Computers don't give me the same fun I get with chemicals. I love working with the rinses and seeing the pictures come up from the blank paper. There's something about watching a picture I've created take shape right in front of my eyes. That's as much of a kick as taking the picture in the first place.

SHE: You're really turned on by this, aren't you?

HE: Can you tell?

SHE: I never thought about taking pictures as such an exciting adventure.

HE: I just wish there was money to be made at it.

SHE: It all comes down to money, doesn't it?

HE: Guess so.

SHE: They tell me that's the reason for most married couples' problems — money.

HE: ...or sex.

SHE: Please!

HE: Money always comes into it... problems in marriage, I mean. I just wish I had saved more, but right now I can barely cover college costs.

SHE: You could take that kid out of college and put him to work.

HE: Oh no! No way! I didn't get that chance. He's staying in college if I have to toss burgers somewhere.

SHE: Maybe your wife could get a job... do something she's always wanted to do.

HE: There's a thought. What do you think she'd like...?

SHE: Maybe she'd like to... uh...

HE: Yes?

SHE: Well, perhaps she'd... uh...

HE: Come on, what would a woman who's been a wife and mother for twenty-some years want to do next? I won't tell.

SHE: There are lots of things...

HE: Go on, tell me, what kind of things?

SHE: She could... uh... take up flying... or go to law school... or run for mayor... or...

HE: And that would help the household economy how? Come on, those things all cost money. Money, money, money! Flying lessons, graduate school, political war chest.

SHE: (Laughs) Or she could buy a slinky black dress and fling herself over a piano.

HE: There's the picture I'd like to snap! Not a bad idea, if you ask me.

SHE: Please, you'll make me blush.

HE: You seem like a very smart lady. And your family is doing okay. Your mother is cared for; your father seems able to take care of himself; your son is taking care of himself; and your husband...

SHE: Ah, there's the problem. He's busy chasing rainbows.

HE: Maybe it's time you started chasing a few rainbows yourself.

SHE: (Looking at his controls) Time for another heart check. Grab the handles.

HE: Kinda bossy, aren't you.

SHE: Bossy? Maybe that's part of being a wife — bossing the boss.

HE: Oh, your husband is the boss.

SHE: He thinks he is. That's the important part.

HE: So what does *he* want you to do, now that you're off the hook as a working mother?

SHE: I'm not sure. Sometimes I think he wants me to continue mothering him. Sometimes… I'm not sure.

HE: Have you ever asked him? Most of us guys don't appreciate being mothered. We get enough of that from our own mothers. As for mine? She quit bossing me when Dad died. I missed it for a while, then she started the complaining. I think I'd rather have her bossy.

SHE: (Points) Check out those two — about your age, I guess.

HE: And yours, if you don't mind me pointing that out. They look out of place here. This gym seems mostly filled with kids and old folks.

SHE: Probably because most people your age — our age — are at work. Look, they're holding hands as they walk together. Good pace. They've been doing this for a while. I've seen them before; they seem to be regulars. The family that walks together…

HE: Nice thought. My guess is they have a house full of teenagers and this is the only time they can get away and talk to each other.

SHE: Could be. (Pause.) Couples can… drift apart… forget each other in the craziness of daily life.

HE: That's the truth. (Points) Will you look at that!

SHE: Whoa! That teenager looks like she's running for the Olympics. Check the speed! My son could've been a professional athlete. He ran the mile in high school and set records. I wish he had gone on with sports. He played baseball too.

HE: Pitcher? Catcher?

SHE: Outfield.

HE: Well that's okay. Sports is as risky as music, wouldn't you say? The kid preferred music, obviously. Whichever he chose, my guess is you'd be critical. You probably...

SHE: (Angry) Critical? You don't know that! I don't criticize my children. Dammit, you weren't there. I'm not a nag! I encourage them. I try to show them direction, be a guide. You have no right to...

HE: Sorry! Cheez, I didn't mean to get you all riled up.

SHE: Well you did. I don't like being told I'm a bad mother. You can call me many things, but don't call me that!

HE: Sorry.   [Silence.]

SHE: You seem to be breathing hard. You all right?

HE: Oh sure. Just not used to these machines. A smoker for too long. I'm all right.

SHE: But you've quit... smoking. Try slowing your pace a bit — that button over there. That's the one. Take a deep breath. Is that better?

HE: (Deep breath.) Yeah, thanks. That *is* better. (Pause. Points) Do you think those two — the hand holders — have been married long?

SHE: It's possible they met here, you know. They may not even be married... to each other. It wouldn't be the first time that... (SHE looks away.)

HE: Ah no. How can you think that way?

SHE: I'm a woman.

HE: I noticed.

SHE: If you came to a place like this and met someone that strikes your fancy, wouldn't you keep coming back?

HE: No. Hell no! You keep coming back. Have you met someone who…

SHE: If I had, I wouldn't tell you. (Pause.) Well, I haven't. I come just for the peace and quiet. Nobody bothers you here… except… (she looks at him)

HE: So you come to get away from your empty house?

SHE: Not exactly. More like getting away from one filled to overflowing with a… husband.

HE: Sorry, maybe I should just be quiet and pedal.

SHE: Maybe. But I like the talk. It's kind of nice, makes the workout go faster.

HE: *Workout.* Nice word. Physical exercise feels like a way to make anything possible, to kinda *work out* the kinks — all of them. Get it?

SHE: Yes. I get it. Talking helps. Or maybe it's the endorphins… or whatever.

[Silence.]

HE: There's more you may need to know about me.

SHE: Yes? I already know about your freaky mother and your financial woes and your shaky business plans.

HE: You make it sound like I'm a failure at everything.

SHE: I'm sorry. I didn't mean it that way. But that's what you told me. Your wife complains about the lack of money and your preoccupation with your photography and your mother just complains.

HE: Which makes it sound like I've failed at everything, being a son, a husband… and, to hear my sons talk, a father.

SHE: I'm sorry, I didn't mean…

HE: Of course you did. You can see what a frickin' failure I am. I have a wife who is left with just me. I have one son in college, and a son who is following his heart — both doing what makes them happy... something I've always wanted to do, but can't because I can't afford to, because my money won't reach all that far and because... because... Crap! I'm a failure at everything.

SHE: Don't be so hard on yourself. You're doing the best you can.

HE: But if I can't succeed at something... just for me... how the hell can I help anybody else? It's not like I have many more years. Jeez, I'm nearly 60!

SHE: I thought you said 53. Maybe it's time to take a step back and look at other ways to do this. Your wife going back to work would be one possibility. (Pause.) You said there was something else.

HE: Maybe now isn't the best time...

SHE: You think you'll have another chance? (Grins)

HE: Maybe. Maybe I'm learning that time is short.

SHE: You mean because your father died at your age?

HE: In a way. My chances have recently gotten worse. You've noticed my shortness of breath...

SHE: Yes...

HE: There's a reason... more than just...

SHE: Something wrong? Have you seen a doctor?

HE: My regular checkup... last week.

SHE: And?

HE: Seems there *is* something wrong. But you never know with these things. Sometimes they're wrong, the doctors, they get things wrong and...

[SHE stops pedaling.]

SHE: So, what did they tell you?

HE: I have a… uh… kinda node… on one lung. They took X-rays and found a kinda dark spot. It could be nothing!

SHE: And it could be… oh god, I'm so sorry. Doctors have been wrong before. Find another one. Did you ask…? Why didn't you tell me?

HE: I just did.

SHE: I mean… why didn't you tell me then?

HE: I couldn't! You had so much on your mind, the boys gone, me giving you a headache, your restlessness… I just couldn't…

SHE: You should have. Maybe the doctor's wrong. Maybe they'll look at it again in a few weeks and it'll be gone. Maybe…

HE: Please. This is *my* concern. You have worries of your own. After all, you still haven't told me what you'd like to do, that is, if you decide to go to work.

SHE: You know, my sweet. I'm beginning to think it's time to seriously consider that black slinky gown and the lounge job. What do you say?

HE: Yes! I'm beginning to think seriously about that gown too. Let's go home.

[They shut off the machines and climb down.

HE takes her hand and they walk away.]

SHE: (Quietly) I never knew you couldn't sing.

[CURTAIN]

THE DAISY WALL
A one-act play
Copyright ©2001

CAST:
THE WITCHES

FRANCINE. 40-ish. The motherly type, caretaker. She is the voice of reason who keeps things together.

CLARICE: in her late 20s. The historian. Keeps journals. Writes everything down. Is methodic, analytical, even-tempered.

ENOIS: 19. Has been in the business since she was 14. The comedian who loves to sing and dance and entertain her "sisters." She plays the autoharp (or guitar).

MARCELLA: mid-thirties. The tragedian who foretells doom. She is the gardener/winemaker who finds solace in the earth, the stars, and the wine.

LIVI: mid-20s. The artist who draws daisies. She sees into a person's psyche and understands people's motives and is content to let them be. She sees the spiritual.

THE MEN: A few in German uniforms appearing faceless.

LT. ERNST GOTTFRIED. Mid-40s. Blustery, proud, in command. Typical military man, giving orders.

SGT. KARL SCHROEDER. Late 20s. Takes life as it comes, obediently. Daring, uncommitted, uncaring.

PVT. HELMUT HOFFER. 18. Out for a good time, no matter who it hurts. Dangerous, brutal.

PVT. RUDY MUELLER. Early 20s. Narcissistic, sure of himself and his prowess. Careless.

DOC — NARRATOR: A doctorly-appearing older man wearing a white coat and a stethoscope.

TIME: July 1940.

PLACE: A remote hilltop compound in southern France that formerly was a nunnery. Stage is divided with the outdoors at Stage Left, a backdrop of blue sky, fields of daisies and height (this is a hilltop). At Stage Right is a cutaway of a parlor with a doorway from outside. The parlor is French 1930s, sparsely furnished with dark sofa, chairs and tables, blank walls, maybe a fireplace. A few religious statues and pictures. The Daisy Wall on Stage Right is angled to be visible to the audience. A door (center) to the kitchen. Another door (right/center) appears to lead to a hallway and the bedrooms.

CURTAIN
[Doc stands alone onstage and addresses the audience]

DOC
You'll hear me referred to as Doc in what you're about to see. As a physician, I conducted research in France in the late 1930s, tracking down the effects of a new virus. This story, set in France during World War II, involves French women of the street and German soldiers. Because there may be a few in the audience who do not understand both French and German, we are telling this story in English. Men are from Germany; Women are from France. Not only do languages between different countries pose problems, but languages between the sexes do too. I am Jewish, therefore you won't see me again until after the war... I mean, the play.

[As the curtain rises LIVI, MARCELLA AND FRANCINE
sit on the hill weaving daisy chains. A pastoral scene.
CLARICE enters from the house Stage Right.]

CLARICE

Doc is gone. His clothes and lab equipment are gone.

LIVI

What do you mean gone?

MARCELLA

I knew it. I knew he'd abandon us. I read it in the cards.

CLARICE

Gone. Even his books and papers. All he left are a few
empty journals.

FRANCINE

All right, stop it. Yes, Clarice is right. Doc has gone. He
heard that the Nazis were arresting Jews. I suspected he'd
leave after we heard that Paris fell. You can't blame him for
wanting to get out before they discover us here.

MARCELLA

What will we do, Franci? Should we leave too?

FRANCINE

Of course not, Marcella. We can't. You realize why we're
here. You know we can't go back. Especially now. We'll just
sit tight.

LIVI

This isn't such a bad place. If nuns could live here, we can
too.

CLARICE

We are not nuns — definitely not nuns.

FRANCINE

Listen to Livi. Why can't we continue to live here? We have
everything we want?

LIVI

(Pouting) Except fun.

CLARICE

Except a life.

MARCELLA

We'll be next. The Germans have taken over everything to the north. Now they'll head here, near the Mediterranean. They'll be here soon — with the full moon.

FRANCINE

Marci, slow down. If they come here... we'll have to do something. (Almost to herself) With Paris gone, I wish we could all sign up for... something... spy work or... message carrying... or... something.

CLARICE

Take a look, girls. Look around. What a beautiful place — sunshine, fresh air, food and water, peace...

LIVI

Too much peace. What will we live on? We have no money.

FRANCINE

We really don't need money, Livi. We have Marcella's garden that Doc set up. Fresh food. We have the chickens and cows that the nuns left. Milk, eggs and cheese. And...

MARCELLA

As if we could live on that weedy patch.

LIVI

Can we live on vegetables and cheese alone?

FRANCINE

Clarice is right. We have the garden. Good food, even wine. Livi has her paints and brushes, and magnificent scenery to paint. Clarice, you have your books and your journals to write in.

MARCELLA

Just like the journals she used to keep track of her "customers."

FRANCINE

Marci, please. Clarice *likes* to keep records. And Enois has her harp, her music... by the way, where is Enois?

LIVI

I saw her over behind the barn. She was yodeling to bring the cows in.

MARCELLA

Yodeling? Oh well, why not? So, do we stay and keep ourselves busy?

FRANCINE

We don't have much choice, Marci. You know we can't move into the village...

LIVI

...or return to Paris. Maybe we ought...

FRANCINE

Maybe we ought to sit down together and look at what's happening. Maybe we can figure out something we can do to help France fight these demons.

CLARICE

Exactly. France is at war...

MARCELLA

Excuse me, France has *lost* the war. France is doomed. The Germans are everywhere.

FRANCINE

Which is why I think it's best to stay here…for now.

LIVI

What about our medicine?

FRANCINE

Don't you remember? Doc said we didn't need the injections anymore. He said the disease is dormant; we're just carriers. He said the green vegetables will keep us healthy and the… er… thing… quiet. Still, we *could* infect people if we were with them…

LIVI

In the Biblical sense, eh Franci?

FRANCINE

Yes, Biblically or otherwise. We can infect people without too much effort. We'd best stay right here… out of the way… and quiet. Maybe the war will be over soon and Doc will come back. Remember, he's working on a cure for us. Maybe he'll find it, and we want to be here when he returns.

MARCELLA

Ever the optimist!

FRANCINE

Better than being the doomsayer.

MARCELLA

I don't say doom. I…

FRANCINE

Really? I can't see how a gardener, a woman of the earth like you, can see doom and death as easily as you do.

MARCELLA

(Sarcastically) A gift, Franci. A gift, my dear.

FRANCINE

So, we're decided? We'll stay here and wait out the war…

LIVI

And Doc's return.

MARCELLA

He's got to come back.

CLARICE

We know he'll return.

FRANCINE

Yes, Doc will be back.

[ENOIS comes running in, breathless, shouting wildly about Germans, soldiers, coming up the hill.]

FRANCINE

Enois! Calm down, what are you saying?

ENOIS

Germans. A bunch of soldiers are climbing up the hill. They have guns and…

LIVI

Oh my god, they've brought the war here already. What will we do now?

MARCELLA

I knew it. The end. They've come to wipe us out. They're going to kill us all in our sleep.

ENOIS

We're not sleeping, dopey.

FRANCINE

Be still! Quiet! We have to think.

CLARICE

We'll talk to them.

ENOIS

With our hands in the air?

CLARICE

They aren't going to just gun us down. They'll want to know what we're doing here.

FRANCINE

We don't tell them. We let them think we just… live here. Like… sisters… like…

LIVI

(Sarcastic) Sisters, yes. Nuns! Yeah. Like they'll buy that!

ENOIS

That's a switch. *They* may buy it, but can *we*?

FRANCINE

We'll have to. So will they. What other reason would a group of women have for living together in this commune? We don't have to look like nuns, but we can behave like them.

[Sounds of men talking come first,
then they appear over the hill
Stage Left/Center, one at a time, guns drawn.]

ENOIS

They're here.

MARCELLA

Oh my god. They are. We're gonna die.

FRANCINE

Shhh! Be still.

[FRANCINE walks toward the soldiers, arms outspread.
The men shoulder their guns at a motion from the
lieutenant.]

FRANCINE

We're unarmed. We have no guns.

LT. GOTTFRIED

Of course.

[GOTTFRIED motions to the men to lower
their weapons, but to keep them ready.]

LT. GOTTFRIED

Are there others here?   [looks around for others.]

FRANCINE

Just us. Five women…meditating.

HOFFER

Wow! Dames. Can you beat that!

LT. GOTTFRIED

Silence, private. Stand back.

SGT. SCHROEDER

We need food. Our patrol is hungry. It's a long way from the village.

[SCHROEDER motions hand to mouth, then points to the town below.]

MARCELLA

Why are you here? Are you going to kill us?

FRANCINE

Marcella!

LT. GOTTFRIED

It's all right, ma'am. Give us food. (Motioning to eat) We won't harm you.

FRANCINE

Clarice, get some bread and cheese — and water.

CLARICE

Not wine?

FRANCINE

No.

[CLARICE leaves. LT. GOTTFRIED motions HOFFER to follow her.]

LT. GOTTFRIED

(To Francine) We're looking for a place for our troops to rest from battle. We saw this castle on the hilltop and…

ENOIS

Did he say castle…?

[FRANCINE speaks very slowly so the Germans can catch a word or two.]

FRANCINE

(To Enois) Hush! (To the men) This is a nunnery, sir. A home for the spiritual, a resting place, yes.

[FRANCINE lays her head on her hands to indicate sleep.]

MUELLER

Well now. I hope I understand what she's saying.

[GOTTFRIED walks toward the buildings, sizes them up, returns to the group.]

LT. GOTTFRIED

Seems you have quite a bit of space here for just a few women. How many are there?

[GOTTFRIED holds up his hand and counts to five.]

FRANCINE

Yes, there are five here. It's getting late in the day. Would your men like to spend the night before returning to the village?

SGT. SCHROEDER

Oh yes. I understood that, Lieutenant. They're inviting us to stay… if it's all right with you.
[MUELLER leers at the women, sizing them up. The lieutenant holds up his arm to keep him in line.]

LT. GOTTFRIED

MUELLER, get HOFFER and check out the buildings back there.

MUELLER

Right, Lieutenant.

[MUELLER enters the house as HOFFER enters from the
kitchen. They march off Center Stage, behind the parlor,
guns ready. The Lieutenant motions the women inside.
CLARICE enters with tray of food and water.
LIVI is painting the sunset.]

LT. GOTTFRIED
(To Clarice) Thank you. And now, ladies, if you will make
yourselves comfortable, we can speak of arrangements.

[GOTTFRIED motions the women to sit.
He stands and paces as he chews on bread, looking around.
LIVI goes to her easel. CLARICE pours more water.]

FRANCINE
We have plenty of room, Lieutenant. Each of your men may
have a separate room.

[FRANCINE indicates the hallway and rooms beyond.]

LT. GOTTFRIED
Men in one wing. You women in another?

[The LIEUTENANT motions togetherness,
men together, women together, for safety.]

FRANCINE
(Points to herself) Francine. I am… uh Sister Francine. This
is Sister Marcella. The one with the food is Sister Clarice.
Sister Livi is painting the sunset. And this is Sister Enois.

[FRANCINE puts a protective arm around ENOIS,
the youngest, to let the soldiers know that she is protected.
All the women don their beatific faces and smile.]

SGT. SCHROEDER

This is our Lieutenant Ernst Gottfried, ma'am. I am Sergeant Karl Schroeder. The men who are searching the buildings are Privates Helmut Hoffer and Rudy Mueller. (He bows and clicks his heels.) Be assured that we are all good Christians and we are at your service.

MARCELLA

How gallant!

FRANCINE

(Frowning at Marcella) Thank you, Sergeant.

LT. GOTTFRIED

(Looking around.) Aah, the view up here is magnificent. You are very fortunate to live in such a beautiful place. (He turns to the sergeant.) Schroeder, are you thinking what I am thinking?

SGT. SCHROEDER

Of course, Lieutenant.

LT. GOTTFRIED

I think we've found it. The perfect place for R & R for our troops, er… officers. A regular Eden.

SGT. SCHROEDER

Of course. Yes. Will you be recommending this to the Commandant?

LT. GOTTFRIED

How many rooms did you say you had?

FRANCINE

How long would the men stay, Lieutenant?

LT. GOTTFRIED
Oh, probably four or five days.

FRANCINE
(Calculating) We could make room for 20 men…
officers… at a time.

[FRANCINE looks sideways at the other women.
They nod slightly.]

FRANCINE
Please understand this would be an im-po-si-tion on us,
Lieutenant, but we can see how important this is to you and
your men. Of course we can accommodate — a few days.

[FRANCINE nods as HOFFER AND MUELLER return.
They indicate they found nothing.]

MUELLER
This is a great place, Lieutenant. Lots of room. There's a
barn out there with hay so there must be cows, a garden
that looks full of food, chickens all over the place, and this
big old house.

FRANCINE ((To MUELLER and HOFFER)
Make yourselves comfortable.

[The lieutenant waves "at ease."
The men shoulder their guns, move toward the sofa and
chairs, removing helmets, jackets and boots.]

FRANCINE
Livi, will you tend to the milking this evening? Marcella,
please bring in enough food for supper. Clarice will help me
in the kitchen. And Enois, will you bring out your harp and

entertain the gentlemen while we prepare the evening meal?

ENOIS

Do you mean…?

FRANCINE

Just sing, Enois. Play the harp and sing.

[ENOIS leaves to get her harp. LIVI and MARCELLA leave to do the milking and harvest vegetables. CLARICE and FRANCINE busy themselves until ENOIS returns. They exchange knowing glances, but say nothing. The soldiers wiggle their toes, stretch and appear to relax. The music begins, stage goes dark. Lights come up; it's nighttime in the parlor. The soldiers rub their full stomachs. FRANCINE AND MARCELLA tend to the lamps. CLARICE writes in her journal. LIVI sits at her easel. MUELLER sits up and eyes ENOIS who is reading. MUELLER walks over to ENOIS.]

MUELLER

And which is your room, Miss…?

ENOIS

Enois. I am Enois. And my room …

FRANCINE

We each have our own rooms, Private. And they are… private. Why do you ask?

MUELLER

(Edgy) You forget, Mother, we haven't…

FRANCINE
(Angry) Why do you call me Mother? I'm not…

MUELLER
(Arrogantly) No, you are the conquered French. And we
are the conquerors!

SGT. SCHROEDER
Enough, Mueller. It doesn't matter where their rooms are. I
know where mine is and I'm heading there right now. I am
bushed.

LT. GOTTFRIED
An excellent idea, Sergeant. That was a long day and a
longer climb. Thank you, gracious ladies, for your
hospitality — a great meal.

FRANCINE
Not at all. Anything else you boys need before you retire?

HOFFER
Well, if you wouldn't mind, would that pretty little thing
there…

LT. GOTTFRIED
Private! That'll be enough. We're going to retire. Thank the
ladies for supper. (To the women) I apologize ma'am for
my men. They have been in the field since Paris.
(FRANCINE nods.)

HOFFER AND MUELLER
(Trying to make up for their rudeness) Thank you, ladies.
The supper was delicious. What time is breakfast?

FRANCINE
Whenever you wake up. We'll have breakfast ready in the
kitchen.

LT. GOTTFRIED

You are very kind.

> [Lights down. Set scene. Lights up.
> Morning, the next day. LIVI is preparing to draw daisies on
> the wall in the parlor as MUELLER, HOFFER
> and SGT. SCHROEDER gather their equipment
> and put on their jackets and helmets. They whistle as they
> move about, seeming happy. The men whisper.]

HOFFER

Did you have company last night, Rudy?

MUELLER

Yes, did you?

HOFFER

You bet. I think it was the young one. If it wasn't, she sure
was... good. Man, could she move!

MUELLER

Do you think they *are* nuns?

SGT. SCHROEDER

Mueller, what did you ask?

MUELLER

Do you think they're nuns?

SGT. SCHROEDER

Well, if they are, they've been here too long.

MUELLER

But they're so young. Or at least, they're not old... you
know, like nuns. Do you think they're witches?

[LT. GOTTFRIED enters from the hallway door.]

LT. GOTTFRIED
Men, are you ready to leave?

HOFFER
Sir, may I ask if you had company last night?

SGT. SCHROEDER
Private, watch your tongue. You are out of line.

MUELLER
You know, Lieutenant… company.

LT. GOTTFRIED
Are you suggesting that these women would…

HOFFER
(Grinning) Yeah! Did they? With you?

LT. GOTTFRIED
Certainly not. (Clears his throat.) That is… of course not!
How could you even think such things?

[HOFFER AND MUELLER leave.
SGT. SCHROEDER sidles over to
LIEUTENANT and whispers.]

SGT. SCHROEDER
Are you sure, Lieutenant. If you weren't visited, then you're
the only one.

LT. GOTTFRIED
Sergeant, you *are* out of line.
[LT. GOTTFRIED smiles, hoists his gun
to his shoulder, and prepares to leave.

MARCELLA enters from the kitchen.]

MARCELLA (to SCHROEDER)
Karl, we have prepared a basket for you and your men to
take back with you to the village.
[FRANCINE enters from the kitchen
and goes to LT. GOTTFRIED.]

FRANCINE
Lieutenant, here's a bit of a treat for you. Do be careful
going down that hill.
[She smiles at him and hands over a bag of goodies.]

[The soldiers leave. The women wave and watch them go.
CLARICE enters the parlor and FRANCINE turns to LIVI.
LIVI is drawing outlines of three daisies on the wall.]

FRANCINE
Livi, what on earth are you doing?

LIVI
Helping Clarice with her record keeping. I'm drawing a
daisy for each one.

FRANCINE
Clarice?

CLARICE
Livi and I decided to keep track of the soldiers. You know,
keep a record of how many there are… or were.

LIVI
That'll tell us how we're doing.

FRANCINE
How *we're* doing?

LIVI

You know, like how many of these Gestapo will be dead in a week's time. You remember what Doc said. The virus should take about a week to finish them off.

CLARICE

We've decided that this is what we can do for the war effort, Franci. We decided to make this a welcome place for those Nazis and to wipe out as many of them as we can.

MARCELLA

I heard one of them call us witches. Well, let's do it. We'll be the Witches...of...Witches of France — purveyors of instant wipe-out for Nazi soldiers.

FRANCINE

Hmmm. (She is silent a moment, deep in thought. She walks across the room to the wall.) Didn't we do all of them? (Three daisies are outlined.)

LIVI

Well, I'm certain that all but the Lieutenant received... ah, should we say, a good treatment?

FRANCINE

(Clears her throat.) Add one more daisy. I heard you leave your rooms. The Lieutenant *did* receive a... ah... treatment.

MARCELLA

Well, Francine. Aren't you a surprise!

FRANCINE

Sorry, Witches. But in war anyone can get hurt. Do you think they suspect?

CLARICE

Of course not. They think they've been entertained royally
by a bunch of nuns.

FRANCINE

Kind of sad. They seemed like good boys.

MARCELLA

Good boys! Ha! They're killers. German killers. Nazis! They
are out to kill Frenchmen and they won't stop there. That
egoist Mueller told me they expect to be sent to Russia
soon. They're out to capture Moscow, can you believe that?

CLARICE

Let me add that to my book. (She writes.) Do you think we
ought to record their names? Or just their rank? Or what.
How much information do you think we ought to write
down?

MARCELLA

All of it. Every last bit of…

[ENOIS enters from door LEFT, half skipping,
weaving a chain of daisies.]

ENOIS

All of what? What's going on?

FRANCINE

Enois, let's go for a walk in the garden.

ENOIS

Uh, well, I just came from there but…

[FRANCINE AND ENOIS go outside
and sit amid the daisies.

> MARCELLA, CLARICE AND LIVI
> remain in living room.]

FRANCINE

Enois, sweet Enois…

ENOIS

Some of my customers didn't call me that, they…

FRANCINE

I know. But you seem so young.

ENOIS

Come on, Franci, I've been in the business for five years.

FRANCINE

But you're only…

ENOIS

I know, 19. Well, I was 14 the first time my mom brought home a… you know… friend. After that, well, she taught me her profession and I carried it on.

FRANCINE

Until you got…

ENOIS

The… disease.

FRANCINE

Doc says he might find a cure, you know.

ENOIS

And where is that good doctor?

FRANCINE

I really expect him to come back… after the war. He won't
forget us. And he knows we're here.

ENOIS

Meanwhile, what if *we* get sick?

FRANCINE

We are sick. We just don't feel it — or show it.

ENOIS

But we can pass it on.

FRANCINE

A week. That's the time it takes for the virus to do its job.

ENOIS

So a week from now Lieutenant Ernst, Sergeant Karl,
Helmut and Rudy will all be dead. (She takes a deep breath,
trying to understand.)

FRANCINE

You know! (Pause. ENOIS nods.) How did you know?

ENOIS

I'm neither blind nor stupid. Why did you leave me out?

FRANCINE

There were only four. You're the youngest, you have more
of a chance if you…. But there'll be more. They'll be
sending more soldiers here from the front to recoup.

ENOIS

I know it doesn't sound like much, but I want to fight in
this war too. If I can put a few soldiers out of commission…
my way… it's better than shooting them…

FRANCINE
(Smiling) And not half so dangerous.

[FRANCINE rises and reaches down for ENOIS' hand.]

FRANCINE
Okay, young lady. You'll have first choice the next round.

[Lights dim with a spot on The Daisy Wall which begins to
fill up — time passing.
Soldiers wearing masks come and go, as if in a dream.
The women smile and dance around them,
hold them a moment,
then send them back down the hill.
More daisies on the wall.]

[Lights up. The women are in the parlor,
waving goodbye to the soldiers.
We see only their backs as they leave.]

MARCELLA
(Turning to the others) Those soldiers were fresh from the
Russian front. I guess it was pretty rough there, but they
won't admit they've lost that battle.

LIVI
They're going to lose their own battles — and soon.

FRANCINE
We don't have to talk about it. We have a couple days
before we have more visitors. Let the Witches of France use
the time to put ourselves back into a decent frame of mind.

CLARICE
God, this war is lasting too long. How long now since Paris
fell? Will the Americans and British ever come to free us?

I'm running out of paper. (She holds up her bulging journal.)

LIVI

And my wall is almost full. How can we ever count them all? I'll have to paint smaller daisies.

FRANCINE

It doesn't matter. They're gone. Out of the war, out of their lives. It doesn't matter. As for us, we survived the streets of Paris, we survived this crazy illness… so far… and, we'll survive a bunch of fascist interlopers.

MARCELLA

You're beginning to sound like me. But I'm getting a good feeling about the end of the war. The cards say it's coming soon. Then the doctor can return and…

ENOIS

And none too soon. I could use a doctor right now.

FRANCINE

Why? What's the matter, dear?

ENOIS

I feel so tired all the time. And I haven't been sleeping well — even when I'm alone.

MARCELLA

You haven't been eating right either. I know. I watch you pick at your food.

FRANCINE

Maybe just a bit off. Marcella, why don't you make some of your great onion soup for Enois. That'll do the trick.

ENOIS
Sounds good, Marci. Would you?

MARCELLA
One pot of onion soup coming up.

[ENOIS exits.
LIVI, FRANCINE AND CLARICE talk quietly.]
[As the focus changes to outdoors, they leave stage.
More daisies are added to the wall. More weeks pass.
MARCELLA AND FRANCINE sit on the knoll outside.]

MARCELLA
Franci, something is very wrong with Enois. She didn't even come down to breakfast today. And yesterday she fell asleep while she was out in the barn. I'm worried about her.

FRANCINE
Me too. I've had to drag her out of bed for a week now. And I can see that she's lost weight.

MARCELLA
My spring herb shoots are up now. Maybe I can make her a treatment to restore her energy.

FRANCINE
You can do that? I didn't realize….

MARCELLA
It comes with knowing the earth and the stars — and putting them together. I'm good at that.

FRANCINE
Well, do what you can. Anything to perk her up.

[LIVI enters, calls to MARCELLA as
FRANCINE goes into the parlor
and leaves by the kitchen door.]

LIVI

Marci, will you read the cards for me? I have to know how
long this war is going to last. I'm running out of space on
the wall.

MARCELLA

Sure, sweetie. Let's go up to my room. Have you noticed
how pale Enois looks lately? I just hope she doesn't have...

LIVI

Symptoms of our disease? Do you think? Doc always said
we are carriers, not...

MARCELLA

But he never said we *couldn't* get full-blown symptoms.

LIVI

What if...?

MARCELLA

We can't even think that.

[Lights dim. Another batch of daisies are added to the wall.
It is nearly filled now.
MARCELLA, FRANCINE AND CLARICE in the parlor
watching as LIVI reaches for a bare spot at the top
and paints a pink daisy]

LIVI

I'm making hers bigger than the others.

MARCELLA

She was so special. Poor little Enois. I hope she's dancing with the gods now and entertaining the angels.

FRANCINE

We knew this could happen. I'm just so sad it happened to that pretty young girl. She was so full of life.

CLARICE

Do I put *her* in the book?

FRANCINE

Of course. You might make the notation at the front. Write down all that happened before Doc left. To all of us. I don't think he kept very good records. Do you remember when they picked you up, Clarice?

CLARICE

It was August 1939. I was working in Nice. They caught me with a lapsed license and sent me to Doc. How about you?

FRANCINE

My license expired in September, but they didn't catch me until October that year. I kinda thought something was wrong with my body, so I didn't sign in for my monthly health checkup. They came after me. Been in the business too long — they missed seeing me every month. (She smiles.) Does anyone remember when Enois joined us?

LIVI

Right after me. I came here in January 1940, almost glad they picked me up. Paris was cold that winter, and the war was getting closer. I think Enois came in March — just before the Germans crossed the line into France.

FRANCINE

I guess they kinda forgot about us after the war got to Paris, and they didn't bother to pick up any others. How did they know we had something special?

MARCELLA

They didn't. I know I felt something was wrong so I didn't check in for my license renewal. When they caught me, they shipped me here. Doc said he was looking for women with no apparent symptoms, but who suspected they were infected. I qualified.

FRANCINE

I'm not so sure we aren't the lucky ones...

LIVI

Except for Enois.

FRANCINE

Yeah. But we're here and when Doc returns...

MARCELLA

If Doc returns.

FRANCINE

He'll come back. And I'll bet he's already found a cure for us. He'll come back. He'll come back.

CLARICE

This isn't such a bad place. Doc arranged for us to be as comfortable as possible. We each have the things we need to be happy — or close to it. I have my journals. Marci has her garden. Livi her paints. Enois had her harp. And Franci...what do you have to make you happy?

[FRANCINE is close to tears. She walks around each of the women, touching this one's hair, patting that one's shoulder, caressing another's face.]

FRANCINE

I have all to take care of. That's enough for me.

[Group hug.]

CLARICE

At least we've been fighting this war as best we can.

LIVI

The *only* way we can.

CLARICE

From my book, over the past three years we have eliminated more than 5,000 German officers. That's quite a record. (CLARICE waves her journal.)

FRANCINE

When you say it like that, it's awesome. We have to have made a dent in their leadership.

LIVI

All you have to do is look at my wall...our wall. A daisy for each one. There have to be at least 5,000 up there. I keep making them smaller as the war gets longer.

MARCELLA

I heard one of the last soldiers say they were being sent to Normandy. I think they're expecting an invasion from Britain. Wouldn't that end this awful mess?

FRANCINE

I hope so. Besides, Livi is running out of wall space.

LIVI

Oh, I could work out space for another dozen or so — way down there in the lower corner. Do I hear boots marching up the hill?

[Lights lower and DOC enters Stage Center. LIVI sits on the hill behind him, fingering her medal.]

DOC

You see, I told you I'd return. There was indeed an invasion in Normandy soon after. It took another 14 months for me to get back to that nunnery on top of the hill. While I hadn't found a cure, I *had* found a way to keep the disease dormant. Alas, I was too late for Francine, Marcella, Clarice, and of course dear sweet Enois. Only Livi remained with her wall of daisies to explain to me what had happened. Upon my recommendation, in July 1946, the Witches of France were awarded the Resistance Medals of Honor from a grateful French government. Livi and I accepted the medals on their behalf — with great pride. Her wall of daisies remains atop that hill as a memorial.

CURTAIN)

SECTION V
CONCLUSIONS

I AM A BOOK

A book says, "Open me. Start here. Believe what you read — because I say so."

I know because I know books. The book unfolds its gifts to support that belief. It may deliver you information, opinions, or a story — sometimes all three.

And not just "a" story, but a very special story, because you chose it and you chose what you wanted it to tell you. Ah, you're a trusting soul. Or maybe you're just inquisitive and in need of something to tell you how to live better, how to feel better, how to make something, or how somebody else does all those things.

Are you seeking a story? What is your pleasure? Truth or fiction? Are you nosy about someone's life and their eccentricities? Do you admire someone and wish to understand what makes them tick? Do you want to know the real story behind newspaper headlines? Just ask a book; it'll tell you.

Stories, especially made-up stories, unfold, don't they? Rather like a flower bud that unfolds, one petal at a time, until the full story is revealed when you read the center, the denouement! Now there's a word! And after all, words are what make reading a priceless gift. For words have no price tag. You can't buy words, like Wheel of Fortune contestants buy vowels. Words are not for sale — at any price.

Words are what shape the story, often told through characters that speak to reader from the pages... excuse me. What did you say?

"What do you know?"

I beg your pardon!

"Hey, I am a book. I can help you with this... er... lecture."

Oh really? Well, I'm an author, and I've known books for a long time. What makes you think...

"Here, what do you see when you look at a book?"

I see words.

"Look closely. Look behind the words and you'll see..."

I'm looking. All I see is paper.

"No, no! Are you blind or something?"

Hey, I'm trying! Wait a minute. I thought I saw...

"What? What do you see?"

For a second there I thought I saw... well, first I saw the marks on the paper, the letters, the words. Then I saw an idea. Yeah! That's what it was, an idea.

"Okay, I think you're getting it. Now look closely again."

Well... um... there's the paper, sure, but if I roll the words around in my head, I get a picture of...

"Yes? Go on."

A picture of... a story. Someone is calling out. Someone else is responding. And something is happening... or going to happen. I wonder...

"Hey, I think you've got it! Wonder! That's what a book is all about. That's what a story does... a book like me, makes you wonder."

Right, but don't stop. Show me more. I want to know what's going on here.

"In a minute. Just want to be sure you can handle this."

Oh yeah? Throw it at me. I can take murder, mayhem, tragedy, sadness, delight, excitement, drama, even a bit of humor if you want, adventure, and, of course, love. I can't wait to see the pictures from beautiful well-chosen words. You draw portraits of people I'd enjoy knowing, or maybe people like I already know, or people I love to hate. And your paintings! Ah, that's where the magic comes in. You draw sights for me from a world I have never visited,.

"It's all yours now. Go to it."

I have a confession to make, Book.

"Yes, my friend. I'm listening."

I confess that sometimes I read…

"Yes? Go on."

Um, I read… just… for… fun!

"Does that tell you something?"

Maybe. But I'd like to hear your thoughts.

"You're a writer. I am told that writers sit down before a blank sheet of paper or a computer screen, whatever — and think, "I'm just itching to get these words out of my head and onto paper. What would I like to read?" And then they write it down, just like they hear it in their heads or their hearts."

You're right, exactly write… oops… right. I didn't think a book would understand a writer like me.

"Oh I do! Scouts honor. Now you know the whole story about where a book like me comes from. I come from you!"

Who would have guessed!

ABOUT THE AUTHOR

If you're awake and an experienced reader, you probably think you know all about the author by now. Good readers get to "know" their favorite authors. Just as good authors can discover much from someone else's words.

Velgen — is both, a good reader of books and a good reader of people. She is never alone as she travels, waits in lines, or reclines in the park on a sunny afternoon. "If there are people around, there are stories around," she believes, and often tells other writers.

Velgen loves to tell stories. She can tell you exactly what was going on in her mother's kitchen on the day she was born. Today she can concoct a story about what is going on in her own kitchen. The stories may not stick to the actual facts of the situation; she'll embellish them by tossing her imagination into the words. But you'll get the idea — and the story.

Velgen also believes that everyone has at least one story that mirrors real life. What's yours? Have you written it or painted it or woven it into cloth as yet? Whatever your chosen creative expression, you don't want to waste another minute without sharing your life — letting the world know you are/were here. Your body may not live forever, but words are eternal.

Order Blank
Cloudbursts

Use this convenient form to order additional copies:
Please print.

Name _____

Address _____

City _____ State _____ Zip Code _____

Phone _____ Email Address _____

_____ copies of book @ $16.95 each   _____
(WA residents add $1.53 sales tax)   _____
Postage & Handling @ $4.52 per book   _____
Total Amount Enclosed $_____

Check / money order payable to: Muddy Puddle Press.
Mail to: Muddy Puddle Press
                PO Box 97124
                Lakewood WA 98497

Visit www.valdumond.com to place your order quickly and
securely through PayPal.
E-book edition available at www.Kindle.com
Email other inquiries to: muddypuddle@live.com
View Val's books at www.Amazon.com/Author

www.ingramcontent.com/pod-product-compliance
Lightning Source LLC
Chambersburg PA
CBHW071133260626
47162CB00003B/776